INSIDE AND ON THE OUTS

INSIDE AND ON THE OUTS

A Young Man's Struggle for Hope

Ryan Harnish

iUniverse, Inc.
New York Bloomington

Inside and on the Outs
A Young Man's Struggle for Hope

iUniverse books may be ordered through booksellers or by contacting:

iUniverse
1663 Liberty Drive
Bloomington, IN 47403
www.iuniverse.com
1-800-Authors (1-800-288-4677)

ISBN: 978-1-4401-9545-7 (pbk)
ISBN: 978-1-4401-9549-5 (cloth)
ISBN: 978-1-4401-9547-1 (ebk)

Printed in the United States of America

iUniverse rev. date: 12/16/2009

Inside And On The Outs is dedicated to those who stuck by me through all of my life's turmoil: my family. Damian, you are my pride and joy. I love you, my son. Grandma, I miss you. I look at those who went before me as guides to who I should be. I also would like to dedicate this book to the thousands of inmates who are not heard. Lastly, I would like to mention a dear friend and mentor. Rich, without you, I never would have imagined I had anything worth saying. Thank you!

The following was written just shortly after my son was born.

Damian:

My son, how proud I am of you at such a young age. I have loved you when you were just a thought.

I would question myself at times, "Am I going to be a good father?"

Perhaps, at the time, fatherhood was a bit new and scary to me. I questioned my ability, but things naturally fall into place when love is there. When you love something or someone, embrace it and enrich it with all your heart. In return, you will receive so much more. Your mother and I, we share that love for you, my son. There will be trials, but my love for you is unconditional. It is a constant you can always count on.

I am sure, by now, you have experienced or can recall some tough times. Do not ever belittle yourself or dwell on such things. Nobody is perfect. As you look back, pick up the pieces, learn, and carry on with your life. Experiences make us who we are. Just aim high; no dream is out of reach. You are capable of so much. In the end; however, it is the little things that matter. Nothing in life is trivial.

I hope by this time you are someone who feels with his heart. There is no real map to guide you, but if you use your head and use those who care about you as a compass, you will be on the right path. You will learn everything else along the way.

Lastly, just remember that all your deeds reflect upon who you will be. With that said, be great, my son.

I will always love you, Damian.

DAD

Chapter 1

Night In The Clink

o o o o o o o o o o o o o o o o o o o o o o o o o o o o o o o o o

"The choices we make dictate the lives we lead; to thine own self be true."

William Shakespeare, Hamlet

How did I get here? What makes my story worth telling? Truth is, I was once just like you. So how did I get in this place? I miss that cool crisp air biting my cheeks as it glides across my skin. When I think of the numbing and the pain that is delivered with each brisk gust, I think freedom. Rather ironic that I can equate pain, bitterness, and cold to reality and freedom. I miss life.

"I can't think about that right now; I must stay focused," I said to myself while staring at the electrons moving through the fluorescent filament encased inside a thick, plastic, indestructible box. It gave a rapid, flickering effect throughout my 8' x 10 foot cell.

As I switched my gaze back from the floor drain nestled within the dirty tile floor back to the stainless steel toilet/sink combo welded to the corner of the concrete wall, I relived the moments that brought me here. Not as if basking in the self-pity that brought me here, or the million dollar question, why and when did my life change to get me here, but reflecting on my arrest as a checklist:

* Did I dump the drugs lying in the kitchen drawer of my 3 bedroom, 2 bathroom ranch resting quietly within, what I refer to as the Brady Bunch neighborhood? Check.
* Did I delete my outgoing/incoming calls and my contact information from my cell phone? Check.

* Did I delete all tracks of my crime? Check. Well, except for the reason I have been arrested.

I worked through the scenarios in my head of all the possible outcomes of this event, each one bringing me to the grim and stark reality of prison time. I had prepared for this moment, as if I had foreseen this event for years now. Actually, that isn't that far from the truth. I knew that the state was coming down on top of me. My whole life, it seems, I have been fighting with them over trivial matters like minor drug offenses and misdemeanors. Yet, nothing is trivial. The whole time the state keeps my file safe-housed within its computers and gathering dust within some dimly lit room inside the courthouse until it resurfaces when I next have some new confrontation with the police.

In some ways, I feel like I am not all at fault for my criminal behavior. I could blame it on a variety of circumstances and factors: police maltreatment, or the fact that the officers have become a part of a system that is less about protecting and serving and more about beefing-up their arrest sheets to get a comfy desk and a higher pay grade. I could blame the courtroom for its lack of human emotion and the lack of thought that is weighed into each decision. Perhaps it is that for too long I slid through the loop holes and the cracks in the system. I could place blame on society's harsh views on dysfunctional families and the labels that have been assigned to me. I could blame a lot, but in the end my family loses. My son is without a father. In the end I lose. I only wish I had the hindsight to see this all coming. I have done everything I could to prepare for this moment. I have started scratching the names I love out of my life and pushing away those things which I hold most valuable to prepare for this moment.

Yet, no matter the preparation, nothing can render you aptly ready to face this moment; because, when those doors slam home to your new cell, that echo rings within every facet, niche, and crevice that your heart has kept hidden away for so many years. It is the prison bell for "let the battle begin." Mentally, emotionally, and physically, no precautions and no measures can prepare you for the war that rages when that door shuts and the cage has every part of you pacing back and forth like a wild animal.

I knew I had covered my bases as best I could. I'd moved the furniture from my house and into my mother's basement a month before, right after I pushed my wife away from me and let the bottle of booze consume my soul with each sip I drank from it. I Couldn't bear to feel anymore. I knew nothing but hate for the world that dared to lock me away from my family, my wife, and my 10 month old boy. I hated the world for the unfair shake I felt I received for most of my life. I hated the world for attempting to play the stacked deck of cards when I began with such a short stack of chips. I packed each dream away inside the box and prepared it for storage at my mother's house. I would hold each keepsake, each picture, each moment and stare into it before laying it to rest. All the possessions I had measured my life by, gone. I put away the crystal stemware, wine glasses shipped over from Czechoslovakia, oriental rugs, paintings, Oxford crystal picture frames, vases and hand crafted pottery, glass end tables and centerpieces, expensive, two-tone silverware and china; it was all gone. My house sat as my heart and soul did. It was an empty shell awaiting sale. My wife was back in her parent's house with my son and seeking a divorce. Everything I had worked so hard to acquire in life had, in just a blink of an eye, vanished.

I lay back on the metal slab cushioned by a half-inch pad, and I reflected. Now, I can relax and worry about me. Everyone has been taken care of. I hadn't brought anyone through this fiery inferno with me. I will be taking this trip alone. I only wish I had been able to make some people proud of me in my lifetime. I am not sure where I went so wrong. Why couldn't I grasp the concept before it was too late?

"What the hell!" I uttered to myself as I refolded the cotton blanket I used as a pillow under my head.

The blanket had served the same purpose time and time again for some other poor soul. It was worn down and stretched so thin that you could look through it as if everything was a metaphor to one's life inside these walls.

"I should have run and just kept on running. Perhaps I could have gotten ahead somehow," I said to myself under one last exhausted breath.

I was just so tired, tired of the lies and the pain. I'd been up for almost a week now smoking blunts, drinking, and keeping it going by putting that soft, dreamy and yet vibrant, white cocaine up my nose. I couldn't think straight anymore. Reality and fantasy seemed to mesh together as I spent my nights going clubbing or to the bars, strip clubs, casinos, and screwing some broad that lived four doors down so I could take her car and bang some playboy bunny who worked tending some upscale bar twenty-five minutes away. Fueling this daze was the fact that, once my wife left, I invited a few guys who remained a constant in my life to live with me. These were more than just some friends. These guys have been creating havoc along side me since I first started getting in trouble in the seventh grade. So when I received the telephone call that the police were after them for a home invasion that led to great bodily harm, I accepted them into my home with open arms. I also took in one friend who had recently been paroled from Galesburg Prison in Illinois.

My head was a mess, and one day ran into the next as I tried to gain some control over my shaky hands and slovenly appearance long enough to put on my suit and drive down to the funeral home where I worked as a licensed mortician. I would work the morning and struggle to make it to lunch. If a call came in, I would pick up a body and make a side trip over to the house where my friends would be crashed out and spewed across the unfurnished home. They momentarily perked up to make sure I wasn't the police and then made their way over to the kitchen to join me for a midday drink.

I am not sure how I got to this point. Perhaps it is like that sensory deprivation I heard about in psychology class in college. There was a study in which a kid's mother asked him to turn down the music, so he did. But at regular intervals, he turned it up one notch allowing the mother's auditory sense to adjust to the fractional increase. Her ears never realized the small raise in volume each time. Eventually, unbeknown to the mother, the music reached its original loud volume.

Maybe, in a similar way, my life and partying had slowly gotten worse, and with each consequence I had been numbed to the true damage accruing. When I finally wanted to adjust the music of my life, the speakers had blown and the damage was irreversible.

But, my life has become a series of ups and downs. My head is running on pure gusts of cocaine relaxed only with smoking a little herb. Days and nights I stayed alive by taking in that sweet, legal, destructible nectar of straight whiskey or bourbon. My insides are now twisted and taut in an emotional upheaval I keep bottled up, ready to just let go. The walls around me are impenetrable, and they seem to be falling down on top of me. My life has been nothing but a disappointment. But retribution is here for those I have done harm to and for those I have shamed. My life is coming full circle. I came into this world with nothing and I shall leave with nothing.

Chapter 2

Parent's Divorce

o o o o o o o o o o o o o o o o o o o o o o o o o o o o o o o

"He who increases knowledge increases sorrow."

Bible

"Your mother and I are splitting up," I heard in a deep bass as my father's voice worked its way through my ears. Yet, my brain could not quite grasp the meaning and finality of the words "splitting up". I looked around to my older brother, Dav, who is three-and-half years older than me. He sat on the adjacent couch inside the family room of our upper class home. I watched as he stared at my father with disgust, and his brown eyes turned to a dark black full of hate and despair. I looked up to this brother. I looked up to him as any younger sibling might his older brother. He was taller and smarter than me. He was the brother that everyone wanted to be on their team when it came to playing ghost in the graveyard with the neighborhood kids.

Then my gaze shifted over to my younger brother. Jason was only sixteen months younger than me. Jason and I had a special relationship growing up. He was not only my brother, but he was my best friend. We would hide in the special hiding places we had found together. We would climb the trees along the river in our backyard and build traps for the make-believe enemies that might try to intrude upon our stash of treasures. Our treasure trove was a wealth of items like alcohol bottles that had floated ashore or got caught up in the driftwood next to the riverbed. We stockpiled them inside our fort, unaware that these bottles held a dangerous escape from this world. We did not know that with each sip, one could be pulled further away from this life. That with each sip it will swallow your soul.

But now, something was different in both Jason and Dav at this moment. Their faces were cold and stoic. Something left each one of us that day. Our childhood was over. Our innocence was gone. Our father was leaving us.

There was something different about the way I handled my parent's divorce. As I retreated back to my room that evening and sat on the edge of my bed, I looked over at the sliding bedroom door that connected Jason's room with mine and saw that there was a glimmer of light underneath the door. He was awake. I wanted to talk to Jason. Together, perhaps, we could figure out a way to remedy this situation.

"I don't get what is really going on. What is the problem? Why are my parents really getting this divorce? Is it a divorce? They simply said, "splitting up". Perhaps they will get back together." I turned these thoughts over and over in my head, uttering them aloud as if God were there to hear my cries and pleas for help.

I knew that Dad would often come home late for dinner on some nights, even later on others. I never completely understood what he did for work, but I knew that when he came home it was questionable what kind of mood he would be in. I would try and wake up early, really early. I wanted to wake up around 5:30 a.m. just so I could catch my father before he went to work when I knew he would be happiest. When he came home, it was routine. We would sit down for dinner at the large room adjacent to the kitchen that overlooked the expansive backyard where the raised deck wrapped around the back of the house. We did this every weekday, if he were home on time. Afterwards, he would retire to his room where he would shower and relax, or retire to his den where he would sit in the dim light working on his computer. I loved my father, but it was fair to say that I didn't know my father. I knew that this "splitting up" was serious. I could tell that this would dramatically impact our lives by the way it was said to us, and the ambiance of the room after the announcement.

"Is this my fault?" I whispered. Tears flowed, tickling my cheek, as they dripped over my nose. My Mom came into my bedroom and held me.

"What's wrong Ryan?" she asked in the same calm and soothing voice that could magically heal the scrapes and bruises that I would acquire sometimes while skateboarding or bike riding around the cul-de-sac up the hill from our house. Yet, it didn't heal this wound. It was not something a band-aid would help. This was something different. My heart was caught up in my throat. My thoughts swam around in my brain like I was having a bad dream. My hands fell from my face and found

their natural place, their home, around my mother. My green eyes glowed brightly from behind the tears As I looked up at her. I was lost for words. I didn't understand, but I wanted to figure it all out. I muttered the only words I could muster between my confusion and tears, "Is it my fault?"

My Mom looked at me and grabbed me by my shoulders, commanding my attention to these important words, "Ryan, it is not your fault." She wrapped me close and she cried. After a minute, she stood up and gathered herself. Mom wiped her blue eyes and left my room. Moments later my younger brother's light would turn off and his bedroom door would quietly close.

Shortly after, we found ourselves in a different place. It was a different atmosphere. My Dad was no longer in our home. Our family dinners boiled down to the bare ingredients: my Mom, Jason, Dav, and me. My brothers and I had therapy. But somehow, I required more intervention. I became more observant, quiet, and indifferent. There was so much I didn't comprehend. I still did not understand how my father, the man whom I loved, could leave me. I didn't understand what could be wrong with this life that I enjoyed so much.

"What is wrong with this family? What is wrong with me? Why does my Dad want to leave me?" I asked the man who sat across from me.

This therapist was supposed to have answers, but he kept them to himself as he listened. Later when I spoke to a woman who was my mother's counselor, I finally got an answer. It was not the answer I was looking for, and it left me with no satisfaction. Instead, that same bitterness and hate that my brothers, Dav and Jason, felt when we first heard the awful news welled up inside me.

This counselor left the room and came back in with my mother.

"Go ahead and tell him," she had said to Mom as she glided her hand from my Mom to me as if motioning for a stampede of bulls to begin. Yet bulls don't come close to the weight that the news would bring down on me.

My Mom replied in a shaky and uncertain voice, "Are you sure?"

"I am sure," the counselor replied confidently. "He needs to hear it."

Mom unloaded the next sentence as if it were as much a burden for her as it was for me to hear, "Your father left me for another woman. It started awhile ago. I've struggled in the past because of some of his relationships."

There was a moment of silence through the room as my mind tried to wrap around the information; the same information that Dav had known for some time now. Everything that provided structure in my

life just collapsed. My family was broken apart and now seemed to take on this often heard label, "dysfunctional." Innocence not only left my life but seemed to have also left the lives of those whom I thought of as perfect. Before this moment, I looked at my parents as people that could do no wrong. Worse, I felt like it was not just that the information had been kept from me, but that I had been lied to; as if there might still be pieces of information that was being kept from me. I looked across the room and just wanted out. I wanted to keep running and never come back to this place in life. Perhaps I would just like to live that perfect lie forever.

So, when the counselor asked how I felt, I looked at my Mom and asked, "What else don't I know? Am I even your son?"

Chapter 3

Arrested And Cuffed

o o o o o o o o o o o o o o o o o o o o o o o o o o o o o o o o o

I am a dream-catcher. A maze of confusion spun within; and my bead enclosed with a feather to begin.

Ryan Harnish

"What time is it?" I groggily said to myself, hungry, exhausted, and unsure what time it is. "Jesus Christ, can someone turn off the frigging lights!" I grumbled under my breath.

I was waiting for questioning by some detective who happened to be friends with the brothers who own the funeral home where I was working. It was only yesterday that I had been brought into the police station here, a three- or four-story building that takes up a full city block. I was brought in by some cop when I voluntarily gave myself up. I was tired of dodging the law, and I knew that my life was coming to an end.

It all started when I was with my son, Damian, at Mom's house. I had been talking with Dav about leaving Illinois and escaping to New Jersey to get away from the prison time quickly approaching. In fact, I had skipped not one, but two pending court cases whose dates had long expired. I had been trying to save up some cash to run and cover some moving expenses before the law converged upon me. I was okay with the fact that I would leave my son and his mother. I guess it is kind of like that old saying, "like father, like son." I just wanted my life back. I realized I'd made some mistakes and that I had a drinking problem. I just didn't care anymore. I told myself that I could quit drinking if I didn't have to deal with the stresses that drinking had caused for me. Fact is, I had racked up seven DUIs. I didn't see how life would ever get better. Already, at age 25, I felt like the best years of my life were behind me and those years haven't been all that great. Every day seemed to be an act

I played out upon the stage, pretending I am someone I am not. I seem to be two different people.

On the one hand, I am a man that uses females and will do anything and everything that causes immediate gratification and relief from this horrible life. I have friends with whom I have shared most of my life. We share a common bond of broken lives and an intense hate for others, masked only by our drunken smiles, good times, and insane laughter.

I have had to deal with the consequences of that life within the life I have been trying to obtain and feel as though I deserve. Because, on the other hand, this is the life I have been living until the final decree from my court cases:.

In this life I am a husband, a father, a brother, and a son. I have worked myself into a quality position within a funeral home that offers a promising future and business opportunity. I have a house where I hope to raise a family with my wife.

But, I lost all of that. I've forged judge's signatures on court documents indicating that I can drive when I cannot. I have been lying to my employers from the day they hired me, knowing that being completely honest with them would mean I could never land a position within the field I graduated. I was convinced that if I were given my license back and got rid of all my legal troubles, my life would be perfectly lived out in the way I planned. In fact, I just recently met with a funeral home owner in the city where I grew up regarding the purchase of the property and business. My Dad came down to meet with him and crunch out the numbers to decide whether it was a good prospect. We worked out all the arrangements including the name of the business. It was a dream come true! I would own my own funeral home, financing it through the owner for the first five to ten years. At the end of that time, I would seek a loan to purchase the remaining balance. My Mom would be able to retire and work in the office and help with my son's care. I would be free to coach sports or assist in any other activities Damian might get involved with later in life. I could incorporate my own ideas, individualizing funerals to make each one unique to families' desires, while providing exceptional service through the cooperation of a family effort. It would be something everyone would be proud of, and I could leave the business to my son when he was older.

But, my nice suits and my hard work wouldn't stop the courts from proceeding with their plans for me. I was facing eight or more years behind bars. I decided I won't go. I have not worked and acquired all this only to lose it. I need to get out. With the plans Dav and me made and the skipped court dates looming, I sunk to taking money from the funeral home to fund my move to New Jersey. In my mind, I dignified my actions by determining that the money was owed to me. If I had my license, I could have sought out an even higher paying job offering more than the 40k a year I was making. In my mind, I put in more work than the others at the funeral home. I was awakened at all hours of the night to retrieve those that died during hours we were not at the funeral home. I also brought business to them. When my friend died, I was called. I made arrangements for two other families I knew. It was a case of the less fortunate, because of legal troubles and not having a valid driver's license, becoming the unfortunate. Plus, I would be leaving prior to the New Year. Every year, the funeral home owners have a Christmas party and bonuses are handed out. Everyone receives a bonus. Last year my bonus was one thousand dollars. So, with all that to dignify my actions, I opened the top drawer of the office desk and found nearly one thousand dollars in cash pinned to a paid funeral file. I did what came natural to me. I deserved the money. I liked the owners, it wasn't anything personal. In fact, one of the owners and my family were somewhat close and that is how I had gotten my foot in the door for the job. But none of that mattered now. I needed that money. I needed to get away.

It was the week I planned on leaving. I was spending the day with Damian, who was less than a year old. He is my son. He is me. Every time I look at him, I see me reflected back. Not who I am now, but the same me that was innocent and pure, before my parents' divorce. His hair is like mine, a dark brown, but perhaps just a shade lighter. His eyes are blue and full of zest for life. He carries a demeanor about him that is never astray. He is always happy and is curious about the world. I will always see him as this little boy. This boy that made me realize that life is about him. Every parent knows this feeling well. He is also the boy who made it clear to me that history doesn't mirror itself, but that like a stain on a shirt, it sometimes passes through. I became my father. Perhaps this is the way my father felt when he left home.

"Who was it Ryan? Is everything okay?" my Mom said to me as I put my cell phone back in the pocket of my jacket. My face had just gone white.

"It was the funeral home. I have a Spanish-speaking family there to make arrangements," I lied. I picked up my son who was sitting on the milk-colored tile of the kitchen floor. When I looked back at Mom, I saw that she knew something was wrong. Throughout all of my years of being in trouble, my Mom knew when something was wrong. We always had this bond between us; she could just feel when something wasn't right. She would suddenly wake up in the middle of the night when I was arrested or would get an odd feeling about her when I was hurt. This was one of those times. I could see that she knew.

"Mom, I have to go. Will you watch Damian?" I asked as my throat tightened and reality set in on what I was about to do.

Dav was outside with a friend, Tony. I would have him provide the ride back to my place. Mom just looked at me and her eyes sank.

"I am sorry, Mom," I thought to myself. "I am sorry for who I have become."

She just simply said, "Yes." Then, she asked one last question, "Ryan, are you sure you're okay?"

I couldn't reply. She knew; I was lost. I put down Damian… my boy. I put down my life right there on the floor. He stared up at me, uncertain of what was going on, but he could grasp the thick sense of sorrow that loomed about in the air. Crying, he rose up on one foot and, unable to walk yet, he reached out his hands for me to pick him back up in my arms where he felt safe. Damian wanted to be with me. My son wanted to be home. I looked down at him and, had I not closed my heart years ago, I would have cried.

Instead I needed to stay focused. I couldn't stay. The police were looking for me and the funeral home had just called looking for their money. I knew the second they reported the money stolen, the police would run my name through the system and would find that I have warrants out for my arrest.

"I need to go," I said to myself, while looking at Damian as if he somehow understood.

My eyes were filling with tears and the empty void in my heart was aching with an unimaginable pain. So, right there, as my Mom sat and stared at me from the couch in the family room, and as Damian knelt on the floor with outstretched arms, tears in his eyes, and one foot firmly planted on the ground as if to run into my arms, I left. I left out the front door and asked Dav and Tony to take me to my house.

We were halfway there when Dav's cell phone rang. It was Mom. She was afraid. Worse, she was afraid for me and there was nothing I could do to ease her worries. One of the owners of the funeral home called her to explain the situation. I saw Dav's eyes widen. He put down the phone and looked at me through the rear view mirror.

"Ryan, what do you want to do?" he asked as he shrugged his shoulders, almost as a statement of surrender. "We were almost there. You only had to make it another week," Dav noted, as if he knew what was about to come. As we pulled up into my driveway I exited the car saying, "Wait here for just a second." Once inside my house, I played out what I had previously thought out in my head. I ran into the basement and into the computer room where I grabbed seven hundred dollars I had stashed away. I came back upstairs where my two friends sat looking at me with question marks on their faces.

"What's up?" they both said to me.

"It's time, guys. You have to go," I said. "The police are at the funeral home for me."

As I said that, I was burying the evidence of several other checks that were stamped to be cashed. I had taken these a few days earlier in case I got in a bind while on the way to New Jersey and needed some extra cash. I now marked void across the front of them and laid them to rest under a pile of garbage. I made up my mind. I would not be running.

My friend, the one staying at my house because he was wanted by the police for a home invasion that led to great bodily harm, looked at me and said, "Dawg, you ain't planning on going there, is you?"

I just looked at him and said, "I have no choice. I have to go. Do me a favor and get the drugs out of the kitchen and do with them as you please. Get rid of everything."As he nodded in reply, I left my home. I would never see this house from the inside again.

I got back in the car, and without telling him where to go, Dav understood. He just looked at me and said, "Are you sure you want to do this?"

We pulled up under the canopy of the funeral home. Dav offered me a cigarette and Tony reached back to light it. I took in those last savory puffs, knowing that it would be some time before I would taste that sweet aroma again. Perhaps I was half hoping that the cigarette would cause a cancer that would metastasize and kill me right there as I sat awaiting my escort. I stared off while my brother and Tony talked outside. I saw the lights waver across the lot as the squad car entered the parking lot.

"Are you Ryan?" I heard him ask Dav.

Without giving a reply, Dav came over to the car and once again asked me, "Are you sure you're ready?" I nodded, both as an answer to his question and as reassurance to myself that this is it. I just want it all to be over. I am tired of running. I am tired of lying. I am tired of living this life. I exited the car and deleted all information from my cell phone. Dav gave me a hug, knowing that we would not be seeing each other for a long time. Tony shook my hand as a farewell before I walked the twenty feet towards what would be the last days of this life. I walked toward the police officer who had the back door of the squad car open for me. As he guided my head in the car, I looked up to see the owner of the funeral home standing next to the building, watching as I entered the car. I would be leaving this place; the chill of the brisk November air, the smell of snow, and all those things I never took the time to notice or enjoy until now. I would leave this place and enter a new world, a much different world where nothing smells or tastes as sweet. I found myself in this place, in this jail cell, wondering what time it is.

Chapter 4

New House/ New Life

o o o o o o o o o o o o o o o o o o o o o o o o o o o o o o

"A good name is better than precious oil; and the day of death more the day of one's birth."

Bible, Ecclesiastes 7:1

As time crept forward, I found myself in the middle of a new life, a different life within a different place. My family had to leave the place we called home; the neighborhood and the friends. We were uncertain where this new life would take us. We were without our luxuries and our securities. All we had was each other and even that had taken a new route. The time we spent together changed. Jason and I stopped taking our trips to the baseball card shop, and we stopped playing games in the yard. Our home was now up for sale and our childhood with it. Without a place to go, my Mom was running out of time before we would face the cold, hard, reality of having nowhere to live. We were once your typical family. We had once attended a typical church on a typical Sunday, believing in what was only typical for a child. Now our lives were playing out in a different way. Color had left the tapestry of our life and the void was replaced with grief and despair.

Our belief in God deserted us. We now knew that in life bad things happen to good people. Those who make the right choices often do not receive that which they deserve. As the last source of help during these times, my Mom, who now worked two jobs to make ends meet with our new family, went to ask the local Methodist Church for a place to stay. She went there to ask for help and, just possibly, guidance. What she received was a modest house where she would pay a high monthly rent. It was hard for me to see God's work through these times. In this house Jason and

I would share a room on the second floor, sleeping on mattresses on the floor of our bedroom. The only guidance my Mom would receive came from the source where all kids go when they seek direction and a better understanding of their lives; her parents. Her father was my role model after my father left. Even when Dad was around, I was awestruck by Grandpa's wisdom. He had acquired all the non-tangible things that one hopes to acquire during a lifetime. His family filled each waking moment with love and affection. He would always say things that a wise man or a minister would say: "Nothing counts for more than what your name stands for." That was my Mom's Dad. That was my Grandfather, and now he had left us. He died during that same time from kidney cancer. Ever since, my Mom seemed to carry a burden within her heart. She knew he died while still worried about his middle daughter's family. I saw how his death affected my mother. But more than that, I saw how my father, and now, my grandfather, had exited my life. I only knew the pain. I felt abandoned, and for some reason, betrayed by these figures exiting my life. I was determined to never be hurt again. I would put aside those closest to me in order to protect myself from further suffering.

I felt inept in helping my mother through these times. I had no anchor. I was lost in a sea of suffering. I was a young teenager without direction in my life. I was unable to see down the road. I didn't trust what tomorrow would have in store for us. I wanted to become a man, but I was not sure what all that entailed. I could see from my father's actions and through what he treasured, that being a man would mean financially succeeding beyond others. I had learned from my father, though it was not told to me, that a man's character is weighed in riches. That was how I would get his attention. He always had a strong desire to get ahead and achieve success. It isn't the worst attribute to have, but I believe it took him away from us at times. Perhaps it is that he wanted us to have those things that he did not have, or maybe he thought his genetic parents had given him up at birth because of financial troubles. It could have been that he wanted to prove something to his biological parents, that they had made a mistake. Or maybe when his adopted father, my grandpa, committed suicide by choking on the carbon monoxide emitted from his car's exhaust because he couldn't go on without his deceased wife, it may have affected him more than he acknowledged. I don't know, but all I wanted was his acceptance and for him to be proud of me for the man I would try to be.

In the seventh grade, I decided to prove to him that I am someone to recognize... that I am a man. But first, I must find my way in this different world; this new world where nothing seems to smell or taste as sweet.

Chapter 5

A Way Out

o o o o o o o o o o o o o o o o o o o o o o o o o o o o o o o o o

"Oh, why should light be given to the weary, and life to those in misery? They long for death, and it won't come. They search for death more eagerly than for hidden treasure. It is blessed relief when they finally die, when they meet the grave."

Bible, Job 3: 26

I rested my dreary face aside the small opening in the door where bars separated me from the dimly lit hallway and other cells across the way. I could hear the movements of the inmate next door rustle against the concrete wall where countless gang signs and names have been etched. I could barely make out the window at the end of the hall as I angled my head against the steel door to peer down the dimly lit hall. The sky was a dark blue color that was hard to see behind the steel bars in front of the bulletproof window.

"Sun isn't up yet. I'm dying of starvation. I can't keep my hands from shaking. And I can't get any sleep with this damn light flickering," I scowled, talking to myself while balling my hands up into a fist against the concrete wall where dirt has settled into every crack and crevice.

I can remember coming in to lockup with the guy next door to me. He was a scraggly guy who looked well beyond his age. He had an unkempt beard and hair that looks as though it hadn't been washed for weeks. He was in on dope charges. This guy had been jamming the needle in his arms for so long that he could be a voodoo doll. He had this mourning he carried on his face, as if someone had died. If it were up to him, all he would like to do is get off that shit and make his Mom happy. It is fair to say I feel sorry for this particular guy.

Before being placed in our individual cells, we sat together enclosed within the 12 X 12 foot, three-walled cinder block room with the fourth wall made up of bars that electronically opened when the button was pushed from a bulletproof, glass-enclosed control room. Across from it there were several booths with stainless steel stools cemented to the floor where you are called out one by one for your initial intake. Inside the holding cell, there was an adjacent and similar cell for busy nights and for video court. There were formed concrete benches against the wall where the once white-painted surface was now chipped and dirty. The floor was scattered with balls of hair and dust, along with splattered stains where fluids have spilled from bodily orifices or from the food and beverage they deliver from the local Burger King. In the corner is the stainless steel toilet/ sink combo that is welded to the floor. It has started to acquire a white soap-like scum on the inside of the sink from its use. Around the toilet there are fresh urine puddles, adding to the stench of the room from the unclean and booze-riddled bodies of all the detainees being held inside the cell.

I sat there, wearing my black and olive-colored pin-striped suit pants with my shiny black leather shoes, shoe laces removed so that they couldn't be used as a weapon or as a means to hang myself. My buttoned down shirt, now wrinkled and in desperate need of dry cleaning, is partially unbuttoned for some kind of half-ass ventilation I might get in this hell hole. My green eyes have a black hue in them from lack of sleep. My five-o-clock shadow has now turned to a full day's growth about my face and my short military haircut once gelled forward with the front cropped up is now itchy and in disarray. The suit jacket with the scalpel blades in the front pocket had been taken by the police officer when I was brought in, along with my wallet, keys, cigarettes, Movado watch, white gold and diamond wedding ring, and white gold and tiger's eye ring with the inscription "Dad" running along both sides of it. I was broken down to my bare essentials.

After being booked in by the police officer who somehow allowed the seven hundred dollars to be put on my account, I was finger-printed and photographed. Still with the ink fresh on my fingers, I was told to stand in a back room where I was marked at 6'1" and weighed in at 190lbs. I looked straight… flash. Turned to the right… flash. Then I was checked over for tattoos, even though I had informed them that I have none, and brought to the cell I am at now with my bedding in hand.

"Breakfast!" I heard ring off of the corridors of the jail. I turned around from the door, guessing that it was sometime between seven and eight. Not that time really matters at this point. It is not as if I have anything that I am planning on doing today except talk to this detective when he shows up.

There was about a three inch gap between the floor and the steel door which holds me hostage; just enough room for the cop to slide food under the door and avoid any kind of personal confrontation. I picked the French toast sticks and plastic milk bottle off of the floor and sought refuge on my steel bed. I just looked at my food for a second and lost myself again, thinking of the day I met my wife.

We were both attending a very prestigious mortuary college at that time. I'd just returned from having to take three months off due to a poor living arrangement in Chicago. Prior to living in Chicago, I tried another living arrangement with a girl in Arlington Heights, but things went sour when I turned my gaze to her roommate whom I had made a connection with by dealing her a little ecstasy. As I walked into my first day of college in a different graduating class, I immediately spotted her. She stood against the wall in jeans that bore holes about the knees and the back showing her brightly-colored not-so-granny panties. Her blond hair fell over her shoulders. It had recently been bleached and gleamed with streaks of beauty. Her shirt was cut off just above her waist and her navel displayed a piercing and a tattoo of a large, brightly-colored, butterfly. She was perfect, and her athletic body and its flesh kept you staring. Better yet, I heard she was a stripper at some club close to my house. I knew she would be mine. Almost one year later we spent an amazing week in Cancun, Mexico. That trip was romantic and magical. It showed me that she wasn't just a stripper, but a woman trying to make it in a professional world. She said that she had to work at the club to pay her way through college. Allena was different than most girls. She knew how to play her angles, but there was a truth in the way she spoke straight from her heart. It was only six months or so after that trip that we would be engaged to be married. I fell in love with this woman… my wife.

Both of us moved on with life just as we hoped it would unfold. We found jobs within the funeral industry with dreams of acquiring our own funeral home one day. I often helped her with her job on my days off and established enough rapport with that owner that when she gave birth to our son and remained a stay-at-home mother, I was able to start an embalming gig on the side to gain more money. I became a good embalmer over the course of time. I worked on a series of difficult cases ranging from murders, suicides, drowning victims, car crashes, motorcycle accidents, hangings, to cases where the body had been decomposing for weeks. I had my fair share of emotionally exhausting cases as well, like when a boy my son's age died. I was use to these things after my internship at Cook County Morgue in Chicago. But nothing hit home more closely than when I received a telephone call late one night telling me that my friend had died from an overdose. I had known him since the eighth grade. I went to pick his body up after he was found stooped over and face down on his bed inside his parent's home. He had a little girl. He had a family who loved him dearly. But he had people like me that ruined his life. After I picked him up, I moved him over to the table and slowly unzipped the moist black bag where he had been placed that evening. It was him, though I could hardly tell from the purple and marbled effect that appears when the veins turn a deep black color. His face had accumulated fluid and expanded to twice its regular size. His tongue was swollen and clenched between his teeth. His eyes, still open, were swollen and distended past the sockets. The eyes' fluid was seeping down his face, almost giving him a lifelike appearance different from the gross feature of death. I left him on the table.

I retreated upstairs and sat down with his devastated father and sister. I felt so sorry for them. I knew the deceased's brother; he had stayed with me once when the law was looking for him for putting the man who sold his brother dope in the hospital.

I sat through the arrangements with a barrage of thoughts running through my mind. I thought about my days of living in that apartment in Chicago when I was still in Mortuary College. I thought about the day he showed up to talk to my roommate about scoring some heroine and then overdosed on the floor of the apartment.

After trying to resuscitate him for several minutes and with his face blue from the lack of oxygen, I heard my roommate say, "Grab his legs."

I obliged and picked up his legs as my roommate grabbed his wrists and we proceeded to carry him to the back alley when he snapped to reality on the back stairs. It was shortly after that when I overdosed from an accumulation of powder and alcohol and found myself in my boxers sitting in our claw tub with cold water rushing over me and trickling down my face. I saw my roommate leaning close to me about to give me another round of mouth–to-mouth when he realized that I had come back to life. It is an odd feeling, dying and coming back to life. I felt scared and void of any real spiritual experience. It was just dark and I was alone; absent from this life and this world. I wish I could go back to those times and change those experiences. Perhaps I'd try to talk to my friend to prevent him from dying. I wondered if his parents were aware that I almost killed his brother, their only surviving son, when I fell asleep, drunk at the wheel, while cruising down the interstate, throwing the vehicle over the median and into oncoming traffic.

Now that I see where I am, stuck in this jail cell staring at my French toast and my carton of milk, I wish I were the one that died.

"I hate my life," I said to myself as I devoured the French toast sticks. I peeled the top off the milk jug and drank it down in one single gulp. I couldn't stop reflecting on who I had become. It wasn't the only thing reeling in my mind. I looked down at the floor and saw a shiny piece of metal twinkling at me. It was the top to the milk jug I had peeled off. I scratched away at the clear film on top of it so that only the shiny metal remained. I tore an edge off of it and folded it over to make a more durable surface. It was perfect.

"This will do," I uttered. I thought it through and whispered, "Left hand on top when placed in the casket."

With that, I turned over my right hand and started gouging at my wrist. Layer after layer, I peeled at the epidermis until I saw that soft red flesh underneath. I was numb. It was like a drug that could get me out and away from this place. I needed out of this life...

Chapter 6

Life's Smoke Screen

o o o o o o o o o o o o o o o o o o o o o o o o o o o o o o o o o o o

"Cursed be the day of my birth, and cursed be the night I was conceived, let the day be turned to darkness."

Bible, Job 3: 3

Bit by bit I whittled away at that sweet child that once existed. I was in the seventh grade now, and it was time to dish out to this world that which was handed to me... pain. I wanted to get the recognition I deserved, and I wanted to shine so bright that even my father would not be able to find a corner where I wouldn't reflect. I came into school with a small pack of what appeared to be cocaine, though it was not. I tried selling it off for a little extra cash, but one of the kids told on me and I found my way into my first suspension. That incident would have my name ring throughout the school and gained me the recognition, not so much of my father, but of my soon-to-be girlfriend. I cannot remember what punishment was dealt out with that suspension. What I do know is that it couldn't undo the gratification and positive reinforcement I received from getting in trouble. I would equate trouble with popularity, with friends, and with girls.

It is ironic, now that I think about it. I recall sitting in my fifth grade class listening to DARE Officer Gillikan give a presentation to our class about cigarette smoking and drug abuse. He brought in confiscated drugs from that infamous police evidence room that later would be the dream score of a lifetime. He peered around the room with a long, hard silence in his speech and then continued, eyeing each one of us in the class.

"Look to your right. Which one of you will be the one who smokes?" He said in a stern, interrogative tone.

I remember thinking to myself that it would not be me. Hell, you must be an idiot to continue down a path of sure destruction and death. I was in the fifth grade and; furthermore, I was in the drug free class of 2000. But he didn't stop there.

"Now look to your left. Now again look to your right. One of you three will use drugs by the time you graduate high school," he noted in a way that struck us as if we were just administered shock therapy, or as if we had just been condemned to death.

"I will not be one of them," I said to myself.

But in seventh grade, I wasn't thinking of the addicting effects cigarettes impose on people, or the doorway of easy access it would allow for the series of poor choices that would follow afterward. I only thought of one thing, the same thing most seventh graders would think about at that age, getting laid. So, when I was offered a cigarette by this girl, I accepted, thinking that this was my sure shot for sex. Hell, look what a cigar did for Bill Clinton. She would, in turn, introduce me to a life of friends who accepted me and my disdainful outlook on the world. In fact, we all shared the same views. Most of us had come from similar family dilemmas and made similar poor choices. Some had parents that used drugs, and others had been in abusive settings. I had quickly taken on this group of friends as my family. I would even call them my family. They made me happy. They made me feel needed. They made me forget.

I found that magical cure-all for depression... rage. I could find something to quash or enhance that emotion. I found my escape. I went to the basement of a friend's house where his older brother had been growing and crossbreeding different kinds of marijuana to come up with the best strand. I walked over there from my younger brother's baseball game and would come back to catch a ride home before he finished the game. As I entered that basement, I immediately felt as if he had something I wanted. I wasn't sure what it was, but he had this free, uninhibited sense about him. He had weapons in his basement and plants growing all around and a purple two- or three-foot tall bong on the center table. It was as if it were his own kingdom. Not a worry or care in the world. I liked that. I wanted that sense of freedom. I saw each of the guys in the house pull that thick fog of smoke up through the chamber and hold in that sweet, pungent smoke. Then a big cloud of smoke made the basement appear as if it had just caught fire exited their lungs. "It's my turn," I thought to myself, followed immediately by, "I can't do this; I have never done this before."

Yet, everyone seemed to be okay. In fact, they seemed to be better than okay. They had clearly not died from using drugs, and their lives seemed to be great. If using drugs meant I could achieve popularity and their sense of happiness, then I was not letting this pass me by. Besides, I didn't want to be the pussy who doesn't take a hit. I would look like an idiot. I might be ridiculed or maybe they would even take it as an insult.

I put the long funnel up to my mouth and watched the guy light the small bowl at the other end. As I drew in a deep breath, the smoke was pulled through the water and up into the chamber. Then another man pulled out the bowl and in an instant the smoke was intoxicating my lungs and entering my blood stream. I held it in for just seconds before my lungs gasped and I coughed out a mushroom cloud of smoke. Immediately I felt calm. I felt happy and free. I was numb. I fell in love with this drug. I escaped from my place of despair. It propelled me into a new life.

Chapter 7

A Prayer Of Forgiveness

o o o o o o o o o o o o o o o o o o o o o o o o o o o o o o o o o o

"Let that (my birth date) night be blotted off the calendar, never again to be counted among the days of the year, never again to appear among the months. Let that night be barren. Let it have no joy."

Bible, Job 3: 6

With each stroke of my make-shift blade I felt better. It was like my own therapy at work. Blood stained the edge of the blade and my eyes were dilated with anticipation for life's end. I began to drift back on my steel bed and think about the commotion this would stir up around the jail as they hauled me out on the gurney. I propped my blankets up so that my head would be slightly elevated. I knew this would cause the blood to pool away from my head and towards the medial part of my body so I would not bear the marbled effect my friend had worn in death. The stage was set for the final lacerations. I stared at my wrist and at the room around me and I began to pray. I didn't quite pray to God and ask for death to be bestowed upon me. He never heard me before, and I had been sick and tired of this life for sometime. Instead, I prayed to my grandfather and to my aunt and uncle who had died some time ago.

I prayed: "Grandpa and those of you who have passed on, it is me, Ryan. I can't go on anymore. I feel like my life has collapsed upon me. You all had such high hopes for me, and I feel I have let you down. I've lost my way and have strayed too far to make things right. I only want you to be proud of me. I am sorry. Please forgive me."

I glanced around the room, as if I might hear a voice of reason enter the cell. I was alone. Only more thoughts of despair greeted me. I thought of my grandma. When I was six years old I was hit by a pick-up truck along the road. I can still remember some of the moments that followed. I was temporarily blind, and could only feel the pure shock and terror of not knowing where my Mom was. I stood up and ran in a circle and collapsed to the pavement again. When the ambulance arrived, I was strapped down to the gurney to prevent me from moving since blood had been seeping from my ears. They knew right away there had been some sort of brain trauma. My Mom lied about working in a hospital so that she could ride along next to me on the way to the hospital. I remember her voice. She was singing to me. She had mustered up strength to sing to me so that I would relax and stop trying to move. I remember her singing… it was the voice of an angel. I don't recall anything after that; or any experience while I was in the coma. What I know is that the doctors said that a miracle happened that day.

Grandma had been convinced that indeed a miracle had occurred; that I had been touched by God. There was a reason my guardian angel kept me around. She was convinced that I had a purpose in this life.

But I cannot see my purpose; and if this is it, I only ask that God stop the torture. I should have died that day… I wish I had died that day. I stared down at my wrist. The blood had coagulated to stop the bleeding.

"I can't do this. I'm a goddamn coward," I hissed through my teeth.

I can't put Mom through this. I need to find another way; a way that allows Mom to make it through another trauma. I need to find a way to end my life so that my final act is not seen as a selfish decision. Though, I am not sure who is committing the selfish act. Is it the one who wants to leave his terrible life, or is it the person who demands one to remain in an awful life?

I had given up. I let go of the dreams of being successful and of being someone great. I would stick this thing out. I chose to face what was ahead. More importantly, for the time being, I let go of the blade, letting it fall to the floor below.

As the world grew distant and light faded, I thought to myself, "I miss the good times… I miss my family."

Chapter 8

A Mother's Struggle

o o o o o o o o o o o o o o o o o o o o o o o o o o o o o o o o o

"When will it be morning? But the night drags on, and I toss till dawn. My skin is filled with worms and scabs. My flesh breaks open, full of pus."

Bible, Job 7: 4

My transition into this new life and into this new family continued well into the eighth grade. I found enjoyment in life again. I would lie to my Mom about what I was doing and would find new exciting ways to have fun. We would throw rocks on top of the police cars at the police station and steal things from the downtown stores. We would cause mayhem and havoc on the city. Around this time a friend and I lit fire to a house that was under construction by firing roman candles against the exterior of the home. My Mom showed up to retrieve me from police custody and began to realize that I needed more help than she could provide.

Even though I had the opportunity to see my father on the weekends, I stopped contact with him. I didn't need his approval or his involvement in my life. I had my friends for that. My Mom thought I needed some positive male influence in my life, so she asked a teacher and wrestling coach to become a mentor to me. While I rejected his mentoring, he did get me to join the wrestling team. I loved it. I entered the mat for my first match looking to destroy and tear apart my enemy. All the pent up aggression and frustration I had, I unleashed on some poor soul. Best part about it; I was not punished for releasing anger in this arena. I was rewarded for kicking the crap out of some poor unsuspecting kid. Still, I didn't belong to the team. Though I received respect from those on the team, I just didn't fit in. They perceived me, perhaps rightfully so, as a

drug dealer. They looked at me as someone who is good enough to buy drugs from, but not to hang out with. Drugs and trouble had earned me something that I never realized I had until that time. I had power. I could control people by fear and manipulate them with popularity.

My Mom stayed busy with her two jobs, and I would often go to school with her when I was suspended for things like dealing bud on school grounds. She would take me to my court dates for my misdemeanors and smoking charges only to come to the realization of just who I considered my friends. I walked into the court room to find that nearly the entire back third of the gallery held people I knew. Mom didn't know what to do. I think at times she just barely held on by hoping that I would just make it through the day. She would try to talk to me about my choices and my relationships with girls, but her advice fell on deaf ears.

It wasn't that I wanted to intentionally hurt her; I just didn't see how she could give me advice when her life seemed to be hanging by a thread. She did, however, find us a new home on the east side of town where there was a sidewalk and nice middle class homes. Nobody knew that it was outside of her financial means. Nobody saw how she broke her back trying to string days together where she could put a dinner on the table for those who were around. Nobody saw how she spent her nights at the house alone and often in tears, worrying about the safety of her children, in particular, me.

I often came home at night and she would just hug me. I didn't understand why. I knew I hadn't been caught for anything. And I knew that Jason would not do anything to cause trouble. Dav had a good head on his shoulders. Even though he could push the envelope a little and even cause some mischief in high school, you knew he wouldn't find himself in any kind of serious trouble. Yet, she would just hug me. Perhaps it is because she was just glad that I had made it home alive, or maybe it is that she needed a hug herself. My Mom struggled for us… for me. There was so much I never realized about Mom. She was lonely and didn't see much joy in her life. Hell, her father died just one year ago. Mom needed help, and I was not there to help her feel better about her life or make her job as a single parent easier.

It is ironic to think that even through these times, my Mom would always remember me as that little boy and tell me, "Ryan, you were always my boy with the big heart. You always cared about others."

Those days, when I came home and rested my head on that pillow; as I crawled in my bed and the light faded, I would say to myself, "I miss the good times… I miss my family."

Chapter 9

Police Interrogation

o o o o o o o o o o o o o o o o o o o o o o o o o o o o o o o

"The soul would have no rainbow had the eyes no tears."

John Vance Cherey

I awoke to the sound of a key turning the lock to my cell door. I looked on with anticipation, not knowing why my cell door was opening, but ready to welcome whoever might let me out of my mind's circle of hell. It was a female officer. She peered toward the floor and then back to me.

"What happened to your wrist?" she asked, inquiring about whether I had tried committing suicide.

"It happened before I was arrested," I replied in a matter of fact tone. I knew that admitting to a failed attempt at death would bring me only a lengthy stay in a solitary cell where I would be stripped down to bare flesh with nothing but a white hospital gown to keep me warm. Perhaps a regular visit from a shrink would follow; a doctor who would try to peer into my mind by pretending to sympathize with my current situation as if his high figure salary ever gave him a hard day in his life. I knew that the only remedy to problems in jail meant less amenities and time away.

"Those cuts look fresh. You wouldn't be trying to hurt yourself in here, would you? Do you want to talk to someone?" she asked.

"I'm straight." I said, as if this stay were a mere formality that comes with my lifestyle.

She picked up my garbage from that morning's breakfast off the floor, along with the make shift blade. She examined each piece of evidence. She didn't say another word. There was nothing she could do with no admittance on my part. As she left she took another glance around the room and noted the covering of wet strips of toilet paper I had put over the fluorescent light to darken the cell.

"Take those down; they are fire hazards," she demanded, as she turned the key and shut the door to my personal hell.

"Detective Sorbin, please come to the front." I heard the intercom system page. "I know this name," I thought to myself. "Yes, this is the funeral home owner's friend. This is the cop I am waiting for. He'll ask me a few questions before I am finally carted off to Kane County Jail."

I was escorted into an 8 x 8 foot room where everything was white. There was no furniture in the room except for a broken down card table at the side of the room with a chair on either side. I sat down on one of the folding chairs and examined the room to try to find any recording devices and/or cameras that might be inconspicuously mounted up on the walls and ceiling. I only saw a digital clock with the temperature, date and time indicating it was just after noon on November 5, 2006.

Detective Sorbin walked in wearing his regular street clothes and took a seat on the other side of the table. He said very little. He still had the face of a child. He wasn't very intimidating. He had pale skin and short red hair. He was about my size and height. I had assumed that he would be some tough guy who would try and barrage me with a bunch of questions. I would either decide to talk or not talk. In either case, the truth would not be told. I don't like or trust cops. Anything he has to say to me isn't going to change my life.

In fact, they need people like me to feel better about their lives. They need people like me to give them work. That's why they start molding us to be criminals from our first infraction. There are no friendly community cops who want to help you. Do you think the cops know the kids on the street and the situations they are dealing with? Do you think they give kids a chance when they are first brought in? Cops are meant to protect and serve, yet all they do is hand out tickets and make arrests. They won't even help an old lady unlock her car anymore these days. Their community service efforts have disappeared and they, along with the court system, have taken over a parent's role of disciplining.

"Care for something to drink, or a cigarette?" the detective asked while making a mental note of my mannerisms.

"I'll take a smoke," I replied.

"A cigarette," I thought to myself. "I haven't had one of those since I was picked up."

He pulled out a pack of Newports and lit the cigarette for me. I figured this was some kind of tactic while he talked to me, so I made sure to take my drags evenly and in a timely manner. I didn't want to show any indication that I was frustrated, nervous, or guilty based upon the tapping of my foot, fidgeting, or untimely drags off my "square". I recognized this guy from a week earlier when we had a funeral for what must have been his father or father-in-law.

"Why didn't you take me in when you were there at the funeral home a week ago?" I asked.

He looked at me as if surprised that I could recall that day and replied, "I didn't know who you were then."

I looked not at him, but through him, recalling the events leading up to the time when I took the money from the funeral home. The owners wanted us all to take a lie detector test. I wished we all had taken the test so that the owners would find out who the other culprit was that was stealing from them. The lack of action taken when that money disappeared made me feel I would have plenty of time for my escape.

"Were you guys really going to do a lie detector test?" I asked, as if amused by the event. I had assumed it to be a bluff and even told the owners I found it to be a wise move on their part.

"Yeah, we were looking to have a state trooper come out and conduct the test," he said in a half-cocked voice that, to me, implied nothing was for sure.

"That must be pretty costly," I added, trying to catch him on the first lie during what was to be his investigation.

He looked at me, probably questioning who exactly was conducting the "interview in progress," as the sign read on the outside of the door to the room.

"Normally you can tell who is lying before the results even come back," he added, with a change in demeanor. "The funeral home must make a lot of money with the cost of funerals and all the business they do," he noted.

I was unsure where this was going. "Yeah, the owners make a nice coin from that business," I said, as if it were common knowledge that funeral homes make a good chunk of change off the living on the sale of over-priced merchandise for the dead. He stopped. I could see him turning over the gears in his head, deciding what approach to take next.

"They called me and asked me for a favor. I normally don't handle these kinds of cases. I work with people who are in a lot more trouble than you are in right now. I can tell this isn't you. You have made some poor choices and are in a bind right now, but you will get out of this spot. I can tell you aren't a career criminal like the guys down the hall from you. Do you know what they are in here for right now?" He paused for a reply.

I looked around the room and put out the cigarette in a cup half-filled with water.

"I heard them yell down the hallway that SWAT came in to their house. They said they were set-up on some weapons and drug charges or something," I replied.

Detective Sorbin continued, "We got them for armed robbery. Their lives are over, not yours. I can tell by people's demeanor who is bad and who isn't. You are not one of those guys out there. You are a good guy."

He paused again, but I didn't know whether to speak. I wasn't going to admit my guilt. That would knock the legs out from under me and remove any leverage I have in the courts. I knew I had some leverage on my side. I knew that one of the funeral home owner's sons had stolen in the past and was their first suspect. Hell, he may have taken the other money that was missing out of the contribution box and elsewhere. He was my only possible way out of this case. Of course, it didn't help me that I was caught with a couple of blank checks from the funeral home.

The detective had continued, "Ryan, did you take that money from the funeral home?"

I looked up at him and as I drew in a breath, I exhaled saying, "No. I had some checks."

He looked for my motive for taking the money and asked, "Do you like the owners of the funeral home? Did you like working for them?"

I answered honestly when I said, "I do like the owners of the funeral home. I felt bad when this happened. They gave me a shot when they realized who my Mom was."

I think that's when he saw it. He saw that I was gridlocked between two worlds. I did like the owners and everything they had done for me. I did like the life it provided me. I liked that the job allowed me to prosper and even achieve the chance to purchase my own business. I was good at what I did and loved my job. It allowed me to support my wife and son. He looked at the pain in my eyes and in my voice. I think he saw that I was a person struggling to survive.

While I had destroyed my life by drinking and catching seven DUIs; on the other hand, I was in limbo with the courts. I was just getting pounded by the police in their normal fashion of simply handing out arrests and letting the overbooked courts deal with the sentencing. Then the officers get a pat on the back and move one more step closer to a higher pay grade.

Detective Sorbin looked at me and said to me, "I don't know if you realize that I know your Mom. My daughter goes to her school."

I didn't see any reason to acknowledge that comment. Once again, my actions had stained my Mom's life.

"Would you like another cigarette before you return to your cell?" he asked in a friendly manner, as if he were truly sorry that we met under these circumstances.

I looked at him, exhausted and with defeat. I replied, "Thanks, I would love one."

When he came back with another cigarette, he had me sign a blank sheet of paper indicating the statement I had provided. There were no words of wisdom from him, just a simple "take it easy." With that he was gone. I would be transported to Kane County Jail. Just another place. Another experience to tack on to the long list of things that had gone wrong with my life.

Chapter 10

One Long Acid Trip

o o o o o o o o o o o o o o o o o o o o o o o o o o o o o o o

"It is better to spend your time at funerals than at festivals. For you are going to die, and you should think about it while there is still time."

Bible, Ecclesiastes 7: 2

Getting out of the eighth grade, cigarettes were the least of my Mom's concerns. I had tried a long list of things by the time I entered my freshman year. I felt important and needed when I would get a call wondering if I could locate certain drugs. But getting drugs in bulk would prove to be a lucrative business that came with certain downfalls. I would go into the city to obtain sheets of acid or LSD, which would become my favorite drug of choice. I could buy a sheet of gel tabs for two hundred and fifty dollars and cut the red filaments down to ten a strip, sell them off at ten dollars a hit. I could also get a sheet of paper blotters and cut the nice design on the front of the blotter paper you can obtain from any science surplus store and sell those for five dollars a hit. There were one hundred hits to any given sheet of LSD so my profits could chalk up to about five or six hundred dollars even after I gave a couple away to good costumers for their business and ate a handful for my own personal enjoyment.

However, I had to keep two hundred and fifty dollars for my re-up money. The money didn't prove to be the downfall; it was the safe housing of the money that would prove to be the problem. Carrying stacks of cash on you was an open invitation for others who had the same outlook on life that I held. It was the "if you want it simply take it" attitude; the feeling that this was one's due because life had handed you a raw deal.

The first confrontation occurred with an older guy during the school bonfire. I didn't see the dark steel coming around and pounding me on the side of my head. After I picked myself up off the ground, my friends told me he had a piece on him. I had just been pistol-whipped. It would be my first encounter with a gun, and it brought home the realization that I need to carry protection, too.

I avoided a series of busts by mere coincidence and luck. One time there were six of us packed into a two-door, purple, Blazer lined with Jerry Bear stickers screaming for attention. I was well into the best trip I had ever experienced on LSD. The sheer adrenaline and visuals; it was exciting and scary at the same time. As we approached the party we were headed to, we quickly took alarm at the rows of squad cars and the flashing lights bouncing off of the surrounding houses.

"Let's get a closer look," a friend suggested, as if it were an elaborate cat and mouse game. As we rolled past the house, we noticed that a cop car had been tailing us around the block.

"He's going to get us at the stop sign," one of the guys up front indicated. As we approached the stop sign, the cherries lit up.

"Shit!" The driver exclaimed, as she rolled over to the side.

"Everyone be cool," I heard in an alarmed, yet calm voice.

Immediately, I put my cigarette out in the ashtray and attempted to smother it out by covering the ashtray up with my arm, resting it along the window ledge.

I glanced around the car and took notice of the red and blue lights behind as if I had my own personal disco going on. I looked at the Jerry Bears along the windows, watching their tie-dyed little bodies dance around the car. Then I saw the spotlight move across the window.

"Now this is a trip," I thought to myself viewing this light as a miracle summed up only by the chemicals seeping into my brain and causing an elaborate hallucination.

Then I realized, "Damn, it's a frigging flashlight. The damn cop is looking at me through the window."

It was too late to ditch the three hits of acid I still had in my wallet and hoped to sell at the party. I had already tossed the pack of Newports with everyone else's in the back seat since all except the driver were only fifteen.

"Everyone step out of the vehicle." I heard the officer demand.

As we stood along the sidewalk, one officer searched the vehicle while another checked IDs from those of us standing in line. I was the last of the group to have my wallet searched. The three hits were tucked behind a flap. I saw this as my only opportunity. My heart raced. I just knew we were all busted. I took my wallet out and quickly tossed the three hits that were wrapped up in a cellophane wrapper from my cigarette pack into the grass behind me.

"What did you throw?!" the officer barked down the line at me.

I was scared. I knew this was it. I couldn't even talk right. I was at the peak of my acid trip.

I could only stutter my reply back, "I-I-I I didn't d-d do nothing."

The officer raced in front of me and looked at hands that were holding only my wallet. He asked me to step off to the side while he took my wallet and proceeded to check the grass behind me.

"I'm screwed," I thought to myself. Then it was as if a miracle happened. He didn't find the three hits I had tossed away. I stepped back in the line where he searched my wallet, checked my ID, and then shined his flashlight into my eyes.

"What are you on?" he asked me. My pupils must have exploded when he put the light on my eyes. I could barely answer. I was consumed by the rays of light projecting and twirling about from the flashlight.

I replied what seemed to be a decade later, "I-I-I I ain't on n-n nothing."

As he retreated back to the Blazer to talk over with the other officer what his findings were and what to do with us, one of the guys asked him, "What's the big deal? Why are there so many cops at the house?"

The cop turned to him and replied, "We found some cocaine, alcohol, and marijuana at the house. Were you guys planning on going there?"

My friend's reply floored me, but the way he played it so cool with the cop was probably the strategy that let us off the hook.

"We were going to, but now we have to go to this other party instead," he said back to him.

The officer laughed and said, "Where is that one?"

"Like I'm gonna to tell you. I'd like to get some partying in before I have to run from you guys," he smirked. I remember thinking that we were in big trouble. There was no way we were getting out of this one.

I turned to my best friend, Marcello, and said to him, "Sh-sh should I hit him or should I run."

"Be cool," he said back to me. The other officer stood along the side of the vehicle with six packs of smokes in his hands.

"Whose are these?" he asked the group of us. There were six of us and six packs of different brands of smokes. When he said they weren't going to hand out any tickets that evening, everyone readily admitted to their pack of smokes; everyone except me.

He came over to me and said, "So these are your Newports, huh?"

I looked back at him, unwilling to let up, "I-I-I I don't smoke."

"Get out of here, and take this one home," he said, laughing and pointing at me.

It wasn't long after that we were obtaining and delivering all sorts of drugs. We were getting wiki sticks, or marijuana dipped in formaldehyde and laced with PCP or ketamine, from a gang in the city called the Two-Two Boys. We would get quantities of cocaine through a friend's relative who stayed out in a neighborhood in Chicago called Logan Square. Since I had been robbed point blank when we got caught up in the wrong neighborhood where the Vice Lords stayed and a guy raised his cannon up to my chest, we never left without our own pistol. We would often go into the south side of the city to get pills of ecstasy dirt cheap. A friend of mine had a decent connect on grams of black tar opium. For thirty dollars, the neighbor of a friend would cook you up a nice size bag of crystal meth while you wait. We would occasionally try other drugs like Quaaludes or Liquid G. Why not? It was our escape to a different place. Another experience to tack on to the long list of things that had gone wrong with my life.

Chapter 11

County Jail Transport

o o o o o o o o o o o o o o o o o o o o o o o o o o o o o o

"Sorrow is better than laughter, for sadness has a refining influence on us."

Bible, Ecclesiastes 7: 3

I waited for the van to arrive to take me to jail. I knew what to expect, but this time was different. Before I had only spent one night in jail, leaving the following morning as soon as Allena or my Mom posted bail for me. This time, there would be no bail. With court cases in Kane and DuPage Counties, my bail had accumulated close to one million dollars. In order to get out, my family would have to raise ten percent, or one hundred thousand dollars. Eventually, I would end up back here anyway. As I waited, I thought about the finality of this stay.

"What will become of my life?" I asked myself. I knew that as long as my court cases were in limbo, there was still a small shred of hope. "I guess I will just have to wait and see what happens. I will just have to see what jail is like," I decided.

With the first glance of the transfer van my hopes of jail being somehow easy to handle quickly diminished into thoughts of "what the hell have I done to myself?" I stepped to the rear of a large white van. It was the kind of van that has no side windows to see the scenery along your uncomfortable trip. It was the kind of van you might see a carpenter or plumber driving down the road while you head to your favorite restaurant or coffee shop. But there were a couple of major differences. This van had large red, white, and blue letters reading "Kane County Sheriff" along the side.

Inside the van there were no padded cushions or seat warmers for the frosted stainless steel bench that ran along the side of the partitioned rear cabin. It was just scratched up stainless steel where former passengers had taken the shackles that wrapped around their wrists and down to their feet and etched their names and gang signs into the metal. There was a stainless steel partition that ran down the middle of the van separating the left and right sides. Only the rear doors had a caged window, allowing a view of the road behind you. Behind the driver there was solid stainless steel with a small bulletproof glass opening to allow the officer to view the status of the detainees behind him. Sometimes there might be a separate holding area up front and, instead of the bulletproof glass, there would be another stainless steel partition to avoid contact with the inmates sitting in the front of the vehicle who had entered through the side door. Either way, in the very front, there would always be that bulletproof glass where you would watch as the officer relinquished his side arm momentarily into a lockbox behind his seat.

Everything about the van screamed out "violent inmates," making it perfectly clear where you stood. As inmates loaded into the back of the van from the various stops at other police stations, the room in the van became less and less comfortable. Since it was already cold and uncomfortable to begin with, by the end, you were happy to arrive at your final destination just to get out of the damn van. Inmates would slide into one another as the driver hit the gas or stopped. As the van made a turn your knees would buckle against the stainless steel partition in front of you. What made our ride even worse was the fact that we had acquired an arrestee who had been anointed with pepper spray, making his stench almost unbearable. Along the way the ride remained pretty quiet as each one of us reflected in disgust and disbelief on our destination. The only thing that would break the silence was the occasional ramblings of a disgruntled inmate who felt that he had somehow been mistreated or wrongfully arrested. Either way, his bellowing was ill-received as nobody cared, though everyone understood.

This would be the only quiet ride you get in a transfer van. All the other prison rides in the future will be filled with the talking of inmates regarding news from across the correctional center and reminiscing about things from "out in the world." This van, along with its many identical twins, would become the only source of transportation you ever receive while staying at the jail. It would be used for transportation to and from the court house, to other counties, and to the penitentiary on your final ride. For this particular ride, our destination would be the start of a new life, a new beginning at Kane County Jail.

As we pulled up to the jail, we all took notice of the building. For most, this would not be the first, or last, stay. I took notice of its bunker-like appearance. Having spent one night here, I thought I would never come back.

I had also been here before to visit a friend who had done some time. I dropped some money on his books so that he could spend it on commissary items such as ramen noodles and honey buns. We pulled into the garage of the jail where three other vans also sat, unloading similar rounds of inmates.

"Welcome home," I thought as I exited the rear of the van and stared through the windows that looked inside to the jail's receiving area. As quickly as I wanted out of the van, I wanted back in. I wanted my life back. I wanted to take back the things I had done.

Chapter 12

Expelled From High School

o o o o o o o o o o o o o o o o o o o o o o o o o o o o o o o o o

"Eli, Eli, lema sabacthani? ***Which means, My God, my God, why have you forsaken me?"***

Bible, Matthew 27: 46

I came into my freshman year with a reputation. I entered a school of thirty-five hundred or more kids with seniors and upperclassmen recognizing who I was. It was not only the drugs, but our troubles that would follow my friends and me. We would find ourselves being talked about throughout the school. They would tell stories about the things we did. They would talk about how we robbed a convenience store with a fake pistol, about how we would throw rocks at police cars so that they would chase us around. These stories fascinated everyone who heard about them. We constantly found new ways to out-do ourselves. Whether it was smashing the windows of houses, robbing cars and houses, or throwing wild parties, we were the guys that made things happen.

Yet, these "happenings" were not positive. We would find ourselves getting into more trouble. My grades slumped at school. The first half of freshman year, I squeaked by with two and a half credits. I earned three C's, two D's, and one F. I skipped classes to walk across the street to my house where, any time of the day, there would be my friends, those I called my family. They, too, were skipping classes to do drugs or just hang out. I found school to be a social event I never cared to miss. Skip a class or two, maybe; miss a whole day, no.

It was during this time that Jason had some cigarettes somewhere in the house. I don't think he was smoking them. He was too smart and

knew better by watching my life spiraling out of control. He saw the things I was doing and, I think, he missed having a brother and a friend in his life. So, instead, I think he had these cigarettes to sell or give away at school. When my Mom found them, I couldn't stand to have her know that Jason had been corrupted by my actions. Jason was the good one in the family. He always walked a straight line and kept a good head on his shoulders. My Mom had enough to worry about with me. Thinking Jason was in trouble would destroy her. When she confronted me regarding the cigarettes, I looked her square in the eyes and said that they were my cigarettes. I looked out for my brothers. However, out in the world, I only knew how to protect and rule with fear and muscle.

Dav got into role playing games, like the one he had created called Obsidian (similar to Dungeons and Dragons), and he was hanging out with his own group of friends. He had graduated high school, but paved the way for me by fighting the school's policies. There was one dean in particular that hated him so much that when I came into high school he said to me, "You aren't going to make it."

Dav had pissed him off when he decided to wear a dress to school to protest the clothing policy. They tried to suspend him for that spectacle, only to come up against their own inadequate guidelines and policies. Dav was really smart. Too smart to dabble in the things I got into. Still, he too, would skip from time to time.

One time, Dav owed a kid some money and he showed up at our house to collect. Jason answered the door. I sat back and listened to the person ask for Dav. When Jason informed him that he was not home, he threatened Jason. That enraged me. I made one telephone call and soon an entourage of friends was on their way. I then went into the garage for a baseball bat and came out like the original Babe Ruth. I got a hold of the one that threatened my brother and the others sped off in their car.

"Poor guy. Looks like your friends left you for dead, buddy," I said to him.

He had an option at that moment. I would let him collect his money, except that if he took that option it would be spent on a nice hospital bed, or the debt could be forgotten along with his threats to my younger brother. Dav could protect himself and he did. But I had a soft spot for my younger brother, and just as Dav had once protected me, I would protect Jason.

Unfortunately, Jason would soon be left to fend for himself. In the year of '97, my freshman year, I would see on Fox Chicago News that our field had been discovered and burned after police found hundreds of marijuana plants growing outside my friend's house. We would often

pick and dry those plants and take full backpacks into town and sell them. In turn, we would acquire enough money to buy better bags of bud. It was a cycle. Now the circle was broken. Every high has its low, and mine was next.

I was expelled from high school that same year for selling LSD. I had been busted and pulled out of class along with my friend, Marcello. I knew when the dean pulled me out of class that I was done. She brought me into a separate, unoccupied room, and there she had me remove my shoes. I knew exactly who it was that told on me. He, too, would be suspended since they busted him with the acid I sold him. Luckily, the stuff I sold to him wasn't even real. Unfortunately, the stuff I had was real. I sat that day inside the dean's office waiting for my Mom to come from her school and pick me up. I remember her walking in, upset and angry with me. I messed up big time. Authority figures kicked me out of school. I passed into my sophomore year with the same two and a half credits I received the first half of that freshman year. I thought that those same people who are put in a position to guide youth and train them for life had taken away my dreams of going to college. As quickly as I got into this new life, I wanted out. I wanted my old life back. I wanted to take back the things I had done.

Chapter 13

Processed Into County Lock-Up

o o o o o o o o o o o o o o o o o o o o o o o o o o o o o o o o o o o

"I do not believe in a fate that falls on men however they act;
But I do believe in a fate that falls on them unless they act."

Buddha

I was buzzed through the iron clad doors as if walking into a dungeon of the deepest and darkest castle. Everything from the sounds and echoes, to the clamoring of electric locks and the piercing comments the officers sneered, made you feel inhuman and worthless. There were no sweet sounds ever heard throughout the jail. No exit signs lit the caged-in hallways and corridors of this castle. Only dark thoughts and memories that haunt your dreams at night exist in this cold environment.

I marched, as ordered, following the only straight path I had walked for what seemed like a lifetime. When my name was called out, I would leave that yellow line we had been told to stand behind and enter a 12 x 12 foot cell similar to that at the police station.

We were buzzed through a steel bar door that led us into a small 4 x 4 foot opening. On either side was another electric solid steel door that opened up into the 12 x 12 foot holding cell on either side.

Facing out towards the control desk that had buzzed us in, there were only steel bars separating us from the officers. I surveyed the room and took notice of a three inch gap between the door that buzzed me in and the tile floor upon which everything was built. I would wait in this cell until called out to go over the property which was shipped with us from the jail on the night of our arrests. Nothing moves quickly. Everything is handled in slow painful moments of time because time is all we had now. The attitudes of the officers are not caring or respectful. They make it clear that, innocent or guilty you had done wrong, and you are here to be punished in accordance to their law until the courts deem otherwise.

An hour or so went by before I heard my name called to free me from the cage. Not a second later the door slid open and I heard, "Hurry up, get your ass out here!"

I stepped out, still in the unkempt clothes I had been arrested in. It was a daily reminder of the life I was leaving, of the day I walked away from my crying son who was reaching up to me from the kitchen floor. It showed me that even the best of things, like a nice suit, can quickly become dull and dingy. I did as I saw the countless others do when they were called up to the desk. I watched as the officer dumped my property out in front of me on the long desk that wrapped around the room. He cross-checked the information they had on file with the information that corresponded to my ID while asking me other questions like "who should be contacted in case of an emergency?" I figured that wouldn't happen unless they needed to notify your parents or wife that they should contact a funeral home.

As he entered the information into the computer, I saw a window of opportunity. There, on the counter in front of me, was my pack of partially empty Camel cigarettes. I didn't have much time to fidget with the package so I quickly swiped them onto the floor by my feet. "Good, he didn't notice," I thought to myself. I stooped down as if to tie my shoe, but there were no shoe laces. I quickly opened the pack and pulled out four cigarettes and cupped them in my hand. From there I stood up and brought the pack of smokes up in one hand as I slid the four cigarettes into my back pocket with the other hand.

"What the hell are you doing?" he shouted at me.

"Hey, it's worth a try." I said quite honestly.

"Put the pack up here and empty your pockets!" he demanded. "I didn't get anything." I said revealing that there was nothing in my front pockets.

"Go take your shower you stupid idiot!" he barked at me.

I followed the desk around to the far side of the room where I was escorted behind a wall by an officer holding a package the size of my palm containing a small bar of thin hotel-sized soap, a small flexible, not dentist recommended, shank-proof toothbrush, comb, and a small bottle of shampoo. With it he tossed a towel at me and told me to strip down. I put the towel on the bench with the package of toiletries and began taking off my socks and putting them on the bench next to the towel for him to shake out for drugs and/or weapons. Next were the pants. As I slid off my pants, I removed the smokes and slid them underneath the towel waiting on the bench. When I finished stripping down, I was given my next set of instructions.

"Wave your hands through your hair. Flip your ears forward. Show me your hands. Flip your hands over. Raise your arms up. Pick up your feet and show me the bottoms of them. Open your mouth and stick out your tongue. Run your fingers around your gums. Lift up your shit!" He barked out

"What?" I asked not knowing what he meant.

"Your dick, you idiot. Pick up your dick!" he exclaimed. "Now pick your nut sack up. Bend over and spread 'em," he said, before finally letting me take the shower that I desperately needed after not showering for three days.

"Get the clothes you want out of the bin." he said.

After taking a little while to find my exact sizes of orange clothes, including socks, I heard him tell me, "Hurry up, this isn't the mall, you faggot."

After I was dressed in an orange jumpsuit the color of a bright Halloween jack-o-lantern, I entered into the other 12 x 12 foot cell, adjacent to the one I had left. Everyone was identical to one another except for the color of their skin. I received a bracelet with the jail house number I would need to use in order to make telephone calls, verify who I am for visits, and anytime I left the gallery. Before being taken to our decks or galleries, we would each receive a clear plastic duffle bag that would be used as a pillow, containing sheets, blankets, and a change of clothes. These would be prized commodities. Those items you want to accumulate as people move from the decks to either go home or be transferred out to other jails due to overcrowding and temporary placement. With everything I was given, I also had tucked away my most prized possession, my cigarettes. These would provide quick friends on the deck I called home over the next two months.

I was placed on a medium security portion of the jail, a section called the 300's. As I entered the gallery, I took note of its layout. It was a large room with a bottom level where a TV sat that would be turned on daily at 9 a.m. There were several inmate cells. They opened at 5 a.m. and remained locked throughout the day until they opened again at 9 p.m.. There is the center area with tables to eat on, play cards and chess, draw or write on, along with three telephones to call home. Upstairs is a catwalk; on one side are cells similar to the jail cell I stayed in at the police station except that these were meant for one person. Unfortunately, because of overcrowding, they now housed two inmates to each cell. On any given deck, there were thirty or so inmates. That meant thirty inmates all wanting something from you. Thirty personalities to mesh. Thirty pairs of eyes measuring you up, watching your every move and action.

Jail is simple in routine, but dramatic in actions. There were always gangs to deal with; rules and politics that must be handled. I was awakened at 5 a.m. when the cell doors opened. The police would try to enforce the rule that there was no sleeping in the dayroom the 16 hours you were forced to remain there. The only time you were allowed to leave the deck was for a visit. During a visit you were brought into a long 25 x 8 foot room divided by booths where a metal stool was embedded into the carpeted-covered, concrete floor. Across from you was that familiar telephone you see in the movies that is connected to the bulletproof glass. You look through that glass into the hurt faces of your loved ones. I would see my son, Damian, a half dozen times through this glass, painfully withholding the tears that wanted to flow down my face.

His mother, Allena, would bring him in, most of the time along with copies of divorce papers or papers for the sale of the house. The officers then brought them for me to sign and then would give them back to my future ex-wife. Throughout the visit, Damian continued peering at me from the other side.

If seeing family and friends through that bulletproof glass didn't crush your heart in some way, the walk back was filled with an eternity of silence as every inmate reflected on the things said during that time spent in what was, hopefully, a good visit. Those that spent that time arguing, or questioning infidelity, would make the walk and all the days to follow some of the worst moments experienced. As you're told to stand up from the booth and walk away, all you want to do is reach through the glass and hold on to those loved ones and promise them and the world that you are a changed person. In some ways it is true. These experiences, these visits, and the everyday life behind bars have changed you. It forced a different life upon you. Society places a stigma upon you, a label, from the moment you enter this new world. Whether you never viewed yourself as a piece of waste, you now look at yourself in that light. You play your role, the role of an inmate. You look at others the same as you have been looked at and mistreated. You enter into the convict mentality of eat or be eaten.

Upon first entering the deck, I stood in the 8 x 8 foot cage that would soon be unlocked, forcing me to enter this world. Everyone stopped what they were doing. There was a pause in the card and chess games and eyes were drawn momentarily from the television in my direction as everyone looked at me trying to place me within their ranks. They looked to see what markings or tattoos I had; they looked to give them a better understanding, to see who I talked to, and how I carried myself.

I am not sure what their first words would have been if I hadn't broken the silence by first asking, "Does anyone have a light?"

That comment alone made my adjustment to the others around me much easier. It made me not a prey, but someone who had something they wanted. You're nobody in jail or in prison except for what you bring to the table. Most of these guys knew each other from "the world." I came in at a severe disadvantage. I knew nobody. I was not trusted or held in the familiar light that most were regarded because of gang affiliations. I was one of two white guys on the deck. A majority of the deck I was brought on to were of Latino descent. This was their world. I was sent here, but I held no part of this place. I would watch, listen, and learn this new routine and way of life; hell, I had no other options.

Chapter 14

Military School

o o o o o o o o o o o o o o o o o o o o o o o o o o o o o o o

"Great ambition is the passion of a great character. Those endowed with it may perform very good or very bad acts. All depends on the principles which direct them."

Napoleon Bonaparte

"What can I do?" Mom asked in a way that was so deeply felt, it sent chills throughout my body.

She asked me this while sitting with me on the living room sofa, watching me cry into my hands and hiding my face from the world.

"I want out," I said in defeat. I was beaten down. Never in my life did I think that I would be in this position. I had been hit with the reality of what several years of my life had done to me and to those I loved. I had, furthermore, lost the dreams that I held. In the midst of all the chaos and partying, I had always still held onto the belief that I would make it to college and make something of my life.

"What have I done?" I asked of myself as that familiar pain and disbelief came to mind.

That question that my Mom first asked me, "What can I do?" was more than just a question to me. It was a plea for help. She was losing her son. That question resonated through the chambers of her heart. Mom searched for hope in my life; she searched for hope in her life. To this day she admits her next decision was perhaps the hardest choice she has ever had to make. She would give up her son. Even if only temporarily, she would relinquish whatever control she had in my life to another. She had toured the surrounding states. She would visit schools like St. Johns Military Academy in Wisconsin only to be turned away due to my

troubles. She finally found a home for me that would distance my contact with my friends and, momentarily, save my life.

I was accepted into Mexico, Missouri's, Missouri Military Academy. My Dad would drive me down there and I would first undergo a physical transformation. They shaved off the beaded dreads that hung over my eyes. I was seated next to people just like me from all over the world, here for their first time, and for similar reasons.

"I can't do this." I thought to myself watching them take away my identity little by little, handing me the fatigues and uniforms that would become my second skin.

That first year acted merely as social deconstruction. The process starts as soon as the back wheels of your parent's car leave the circle drive and exits the shadow of the administrative building that still holds the strong, but aged look from the day it was first built. On the campus and to one side were the three large barrack houses where we lived inside our 10 x 12 foot rooms shared with another cadet. Our rooms were meticulous in the way they were to be set up. Shoes and clothes all set up orderly and in their proper place. A common bathroom in the center of each hallway throughout the three floors of the building held the toilets and showers where each cadet was to maintain the same cleanliness as one's room ... spotless.

To the other side of the administration building sat the school house. The lower floor of the school housed the kitchen and dining hall where each cadet would take his turn being a waiter and serving the straight-sitting (one fist away from the table) cadets who had marched in formations to the meal to dine.

Next to that dining hall and school house was the medical building where we would line up for medication and receive our mail. In the first year, I also met up with my connect or dealer. It was the highlight of the day.

Everything was routine, structured, and orderly. Every cadet was in JROTC and would learn how to drill with rifles, march, dress, shine shoes, take lacquer off brass buckles and medals neatly pinned to uniforms, and read grid coordinates. I was stuck in this hell hole, relentlessly not giving in to their strict way of life. I would line up for formations, eat, talk, and crap as I was told. Yet, I ached to be home. I missed the laughs and fun times that were stripped away from me. I wasn't able to phone or receive letters from family or friends for one month. That is all it took to have my name and reputation wiped away from the minds and hearts of the community I had left. I was torn away from that world, but I never left my Mom's heart.

After that first month, Mom would receive gut-wrenching calls from me begging to get out of this place. I had undergone a series of challenges. Yet, she held firm, knowing that while it was difficult for both of us, my cries for help were not because of the challenges I was going through, but the changes that were slowly happening. I had lashed out several times, but each time I was defeated.

I had thrown a chair in the chow hall when I was told to remain seated at attention with my arms folded over one another raised twelve inches over the table at a right angle to my body. I am not sure what hurt more, the fact that my arms were tired and numb from the duration of time that had elapsed in that position, or the fact that it was some high ranking cadet that had wielded this power over me. I couldn't take it that these upper classmen waved their rank around like a cop would his badge.

"You're no better than me! Stop acting like the police, you asshole!" I would yell out at them many times.

Only to get their reply back, "And you don't have your Mommy's skirt to hide under anymore!"

For a while life at the military academy was a series of tortures as the demons were pulled and stretched out of me. Though sometimes, these tortures were physically directed as well.

For weeks I had lined up at formation staring straight ahead at the brick wall opposite me fixated on that single spot I had come to know very well. But one time it was different. A cadet who was a sergeant I had beaten in wrestling time and time again would now be the one coming to check our barracks for count and for order. I didn't even see it coming. I heard his voice talking to our platoon leader down the hall for that formation's count, the next thing I knew and felt was the pain soar through my body as I was hit along side my head.

"Stand up, Private! Nobody told you to move!" he yelled as I knelt over in pain, blocking my head and face from what might come next. I looked across from me at another cadet, my friend, who looked down at me but remained at attention with his hands along the seam of his pants.

Each day I wouldn't fight back. Each day I retired back to my room, blood boiling and on the brink of sheer murder. Finally, I would hand him back the torture he dealt to me. I brought a knife tucked in my sock out to formation. I vowed that the next time he hit me and sent me down while covering my eyes, it will be the look of murder I hide as I recoil and send him to the abyss as I lunge in pure hate and revenge. I would unleash a blood bath upon him. I came out that day wanting to kill him;

I was going to kill him. He never realized how close to death he came that day. If only he would have returned to our floor for formation; if he would have kept his job as Orderly one more day.

I had a scrape up with another cadet later when I didn't stand at attention for him as he passed me in the hallway. Even though he had been busted down to private for hazing, and we were now the same rank so I didn't have to go to attention for him, he thought otherwise.

"You stand attention for me when I pass!" he said in his strong Spanish accent. He was a dark-skinned and rather portly senior. He was one, among the many others, who had come from Mexico to seek an education in the United States. He was unaware of my recently interrupted murder plan. He was unaware of the hate I held towards his senior class and their tough police-like attitude. He was unaware what I was going to do to him. He lunged forward landing a hard right hook on the side of my head. Adrenaline ran through me and from that point on, there was no stopping me until the Company Commander, along with several other cadets, pulled me off of him. For a minute, I had basked in the enjoyment of hearing his head "PING" off the wall as I delivered knees and punches into his head. His eye was swollen and his lip was fattened and split. I stood there unashamed of the terror he felt. He deserved every second of it and more in my eyes.

I didn't care for any of them. I didn't care at all. I just wanted to go home. Yet, for each incident of aggression, there was the other more positive side to being at the Academy. My grades improved to B's and C's. I was taking pride in my schoolwork. Eventually, I realized I wasn't going anywhere. My pleas fell on deaf ears. I would have to find my place here among this society. I would be forced to watch, listen, and learn this new routine and way of life; hell, I have no other options.

Chapter 15

Jailhouse Rules

o o o o o o o o o o o o o o o o o o o o o o o o o o o o o o o o o o o

"There is one robber whom the law does not strike at, and who steals what is most precious to men: time."

Napoleon Bonaparte

Some time had passed since the day we broke the plastic covering over the light and twisted pencil lead into the ends of some toilet paper to "pop the light." The light still didn't work but now it served a purpose, not only as a lighter when cigarettes were snatched from an officer's post or from a nurse's pocket, but as a clever hiding spot for other contraband.

I had learned to get along with almost everyone on the deck. I played cards and worked out by doing push-ups off the concrete bench in front of the TV that was encased inside of an indestructible box with bulletproof glass in front of the screen. We would use a towel to do curls off the table, with one person holding a towel taut and providing resistance for the other person.

The food was poor to say the least. A person barely makes the minimum requirement for survival off of what they offer, so doing whatever you can for money is almost necessary for survival. Some may draw portraits, as I did, make cards, offer friendships, gamble, or threaten to get what they need. All this is just another day of life in jail.

Yet things like this indicated some ingenious ideas of prior inmates. It is hard to imagine that someone thought these things up. We made ovens out of the foil part of chip bags and taped them to boxes using labels from deodorant and shampoo bottles. We brewed alcohol using white rice, or the heels of bread that we smashed up and combined with oranges and sugar. Mixed up with some water and using the heat from the lights, in a few weeks of burping out the gases, you have some jailhouse hooch. We made straps out of torn

T-shirts and a torn box to make oven racks held under the light for noodles and cakes made out of smashed honey buns, chocolate, and peanut butter. We were able to "fish" items to another cell while locked down by using a couple methods: if you had bars on your cell door, you could throw your sheet out your cell door while holding onto the other end so the receiving person could try and toss the item onto the sheet. Another method was to pull threads through torn clothing and tie them together to make one long string. Then tie the string around a hole made in a bar of soap or a small book and slide it out your cell door. The other person tried to cross your fishing line with theirs and pull it into their cell where they would tie the item to your fishing line and you reeled it back into your cell.

Everything becomes an easier adjustment after some time goes by, but the hardest thing to adjust to is the attitudes of other inmates. Everyone gets "tried" eventually. There is no way around it. What you do when that time comes depends on who you want to be; what you want to handle. There are rules formed in jail. For example, if you are called a "bitch," you fight. That is calling someone your ho, your property, a mark, a "vic" (short for victim), or as it says, your bitch. If you don't fight, it indicates to others that you are an easy target for ridicule and you won't stick up for yourself when taken advantage of by others. For some, that doesn't matter; but their time is long and hard. If you are disrespected by them throwing down your gang sign, or by "calling you out" using derogatory terms like "faggot," it is another inevitable way to a fight. Sometimes you are measured up other in ways. Wrestling is one of those other avenues of assessment.

When I was pursued by a short, but extremely toned and bulked black guy on my gallery called KC, I saw no other choice but to adhere to his demands. I knew I was a good wrestler, but this is different. Choke-outs, body-shots, and open hand slaps are permitted.

We went down to the lower part of the gallery where there is a large open space. It was perhaps a 12 x 9 foot space with the TV wall, cell doors and formed concrete bench making up three walls. Above the painted brick wall were railings containing the onlookers from the middle portion of the deck, sitting at tables. We had both taken off our shirts so that the contender couldn't use the shirt to grab and thrash the other one about. Most everyone has shaved heads or close cropped hair to offer no advantage to the other person. Plus, jail is a dirty place where many micro-organisms thrive with the insects, and with no clippers or scissors, keeping any other look is hard and costly.

KC stood puffed with pride after beating up the other white boy on the deck. His arms were massive after years of working out in the penitentiary. He rocked back and "whack!" My head jolted off to the side as he smacked my head off its hinges. He rocked another punch brushing the side of my stomach.

"Shit! I'm gonna die." I thought to myself, looking at the sheer size of KC. Then I saw it, KC was nowhere to be seen. He ducked down reaching for my legs to pick me up and body slam me against the hard linoleum floor. I threw my legs back and sprawled on top of him wrapping one arm around his head and prying the other from under his arm snapping him onto his back.

"I got you, nigga!" I said proudly as I switched over to a head-lock, almost choking every breath out of him and not letting go for dear life. I looked up and saw the awe of the other guys on the deck.

"Alright nigga…" he said valiantly, giving up and shaking hands with me afterwards as a sign of respect.

That secured my position on the deck. I had proven myself and showed that I just wouldn't cave-in to someone. I didn't want to, and I was scared shitless, but some things are worth fighting over. My livelihood was worth fighting over. Time and time again the other white boy would cave-in to pressures and threats, not doing anything but ducking his head in shame. He went through torment every day. His cell was invaded night after night as people took it over to play dice and take his food. Every day he would have fresh bruises and marks of defeat and disappointment.

Nobody would reach out to help him, each inmate is on his own. Nobody wants to be a "hero" and stick up for someone else and subject themselves to the same treatment. You come in and quickly are made aware of the rules. How you live up to them is up to you. I couldn't be soft in this environment. I couldn't think of Damian and act as a father or as a loved family member. My accomplishments meant nothing in here. It isn't the way of life here. I needed to let myself be that hardened criminal; a convict. I needed to create myself and drop the "I'm a good guy" routine. So I did. I chose to drop the act. I needed to fall into place and move on with life, keeping my eyes open.

Chapter 16

An Act Played By A Fool

o o o o o o o o o o o o o o o o o o o o o o o o o o o o o o o o o o o

"You must be the change you wish to see in the world."

Mohandas Gandhi

"Nothing you say matters without proof or evidence," my English teacher, who was a master sergeant in the Marines during the Vietnam War, said to our class. He finished off with a phrase that stuck with me, "One's actions will measure the success or failure of one's character."

He was explaining to us that without study or substantial knowledge on a subject, our words fall upon deaf ears. His words had a way of moving the class, particularly me. The medals attached to his uniform spoke volumes to us. He was adorned with colors one could only dream of achieving during a military career. For me, one stood out more than the others. It was the color of royalty, a color rarely found in nature. He wore multiple purple hearts for injuries sustained during battle. This was a man that knew what he spoke about. A man that took everything the world had to offer and still found beauty within it. He introduced me to the hidden signs and meanings of things. It was because of him I fell in love with poetry and, more importantly, school.

I struggled to find the beauty in life. I had missed all the signs presented to me. I wanted to be heard. I wanted my existence to matter. However, I had achieved nothing except negative attention based on my actions. My homecoming over the holidays revealed that my friends didn't miss me or care about where I had been. I sought attention from my younger brother's friends who idolized me from my past actions. I would use that reputation to find girls.

However something changed during the time I was gone. My hometown was overcome by a new epidemic; an epidemic known as heroin. I would hear that people I had known were dying. One was left for dead at a hotel party where friends made an anonymous telephone call to the police saying they discovered a dead body lying face down on the hotel bed. His eyes were open and unseeing; his tongue clenched between his teeth as he struggled for that last breath, unwilling to face the inevitable. His body was fixed in the manner in which he died. The syringe still plunged into the arm dangling from his body causing the post mortem stain to settle in. The skin slid off of his arm as the paramedics tried to grab it to move him on to a solid surface to open airways and check vitals. He died alone. His friends left him there with no chance that he could make it home and rectify the mistakes that led to his death. Perhaps a kiss to his mother followed by the sweet words, "I love you, Mom. See you in the morning."

I saw actions speak volumes when I came home over Christmas break to attend an old friend's funeral. He had died after crashing his car into an embankment and pole. He was killed instantly. He had attended a party at a familiar house out west of town. The person he was with endured minor amnesia but suffered greatly at the expense of his friend's death. As I drove up to the funeral home where I would later briefly work, I noticed all the cars and lives he touched while alive. He left this world prematurely. But in his lifestyle, people don't last long. I saw friends saddened and acting emotionally unsound. His parents were in the front row on the couches that sat ahead of the folding chairs facing the casket. Lying below the colored lights shining down on him to mask the defects of make-up and marks that couldn't be covered up was their son. I watched as people cried audibly and demonstrated their sadness by acts of small violent outbursts. It wasn't that they weren't sad, but all I could think of was that this was all an act. That soon things would carry on just as they had in the past and that day would be forgotten. However, there was someone there who would never forget the day they received that awful telephone call. Those people are his parents; his family. That day will mark misery for them for the rest of their days. The playback of his life would leave them feeling unfulfilled. Family doesn't just move past those times. They never really heal. They just learn how to carry on. Of course, we cared about him. We just could not compare the depths of our feeling to the emotions of family. We disgraced ourselves as we thought selfishly about how he would be remembered and what he would want if he were alive for another five minutes. We did not think he would like to say goodbye to his parents. We didn't think of how his parent's must feel.

Instead of thinking his last five minutes, if chosen, would be to spend it with his parents, we thought only of ourselves by throwing various drug paraphernalia along side him in the casket. This last act erased him from our life. And, like the half-dozen friends who would die in various ways in the following year, he was rarely ever spoken about again.

When I went back to military school, I decided that there was more to this life. I moved forward. I would let my friends be a preamble for my life. I chose to succeed in military school, move up through the ranks, and change my life. I chose to drop the act. I needed to fall into place and move on with this life, keeping my eyes open.

Chapter 17

Overcrowded For The Holiday

o o o o o o o o o o o o o o o o o o o o o o o o o o o o o o o o o o o o o o o o o

"All this worldly wisdom was once the unamiable heresy of some wise man."

Henry David Thoreau

Not long after the wrestling match against KC, I heard my name get called over the gallery from the cage up front.

"Harnish, pack your shit! You're going to Henry County!" The officer barked at me.

I had just placed my commissary order for that month. My Mom would send money for my books so that I could get what I needed from the commissary and even mix a little of it up every now and then playing squares or gambling on sports and cards. I hadn't heard from Dav much since he had moved out of the house. Dav provided me with information regarding my case, often giving me a false sense of hope. He knew that hope wears thin behind these walls, but even a false sense of hope is still reason to move forward. Plus, on the phone with him, I was able to talk shit about things even I knew weren't true. I would say things loud enough to play into the hands of others, solidifying my part on the deck. Everybody amplifies their roles outside of these walls to personify who they are within these walls. Hell, how are you going to disprove it?

Jason and his girlfriend, Maggie, stopped by a couple times for visits and brought my son. It helps to have those who care for you stop by and show you that you still exist for them. There are times that you wonder whether people beyond this jail ever think about you at all. Sometimes it is the bad news that lets you know people are still alive.

I had been worried about calling my Dad, wondering what he might think about his son behind bars. I told him just prior to getting picked up that I was in some trouble and had been thinking about leaving. I was in such a mess I didn't know who to turn to or what to do. I went to the only people that I felt knew me. Since then, that contact I so desperately needed and wanted from the world, was the same contact I feared. I wondered whether a "click" on the other end or a message saying, "your call was not accepted," would be the last and only words I would hear connected to my father.

But now, I was placed inside of Henry County Jail, some three hours away from home. I was on a block known inside as the "God Block" because prayers were spoken before each meal and lock down at night. This place was different. You could come and go out of your cell as you pleased. You could visit other cells, too. The food was much better, the jail was clean and empty beds still existed among the galleries. Most of the inmates were there on FED cases. They were looking at doing 85% of the time they would probably be sentenced to with over a 90% conviction rate. Only one county that I know of beats that percentage, and that is DuPage County. Otherwise, it was country out here. The only other thing that people tended to get arrested for was manufacturing and delivery of crystal meth. The county was handing out what seemed like death sentences for that stuff. One guy three cells down from me had received more than ten years for his first offense. He got caught with crystal meth for his own personal use. That kind of sentence was unheard of where I lived. I guess that was the down side about being in a jail where nobody is "tried" and people are whipped down and afraid of doing anything that might draw police attention. I had my own down side there.

I waited anxiously for the other line to pick up so that I could talk to my Mom. I hadn't spoken to her for some time now. Every now and then I felt like I was getting too tied up in matters that would make me weak, so I would cease contact for a while from the outside world.

"Thank you," I heard the robotic, female, voice say on the other line, thanking me for a telephone call that makes it perfectly clear that speech is not free in this world. Each telephone call was something like three dollars or more for the first minute and nearly fifty cents for each additional minute. This made telephone calls to my ex-wife nearly impossible since she had been out of a job and was busy raising our son.

"Ryan, how are you doing?" my mom said, hinting at a bit of pain as her voice seemed to tremble through the phone.

"I am okay. Right now I am in Henry County since Kane is overcrowded." I said in my most upbeat voice. "I tried to reach you for a couple days now. Everything all right?"

There was a moment of silence that seemed to say it all. Something was wrong. I wondered what it could be. Who it could have been?

"Everything is going to be okay. Damian is in the hospital after he spiked a high temperature of 103 degrees. He was put on oxygen to help him breathe and he struggled for a while, but it seems like he will pull through okay," she said, trying to sound as hopeful as I did even when things were not as good as you made them seem.

"I have to go Mom. I-I I just gotta go. I will call you in few days for Christmas."

As inmates prayed and people laughed, I stayed inside my room, denying God's existence and cursing him for my life. I found those days to be my worst days in jail. It hit me harder than any inmate could. I did nothing but work out, eat, and curse this holiday season. I wouldn't feel better until I spoke with Mom again after Christmas. She came for a visit. We talked and looked at one another through a television screen, anxious for the day when we could just hold each other again.

A month had gone by. It was sometime in January when they took me on the drive three hours back to Kane County Jail. I liked it back there. The boring routine and lack of excitement made me happy to be back. Plus, I would be able to join up with my deck and see those familiar faces I had come to know.

As I walked towards the 300s back home to my medium security wing, I heard someone call out, "Stop! Where the hell do you think you're going?"

I turned to see an officer coming toward me from an unfamiliar part of the jail behind a secured entrance.

"Open 500," the officer said into his walkie-talkie while three tactical training team members came barraging my direction yelling, "Put your shit on the ground and kiss the damn wall!"

"What the hell! What you doin' man?!" I yelled back, used to this treatment, but never before face to face with pepper bullet guns pointed at my face.

"Where the hell do you belong?" he said to me now.

"300s..." I said, questioning now whether I would be returning or what had happened while I was gone.

"He's the one," the guard indicated to the other officer beside him.

Then I heard another officer step up behind me and say, "You plugged?" This is a common way of asking if you belong to a gang. Now I knew I wouldn't be going back to the 300s. They only ask you this question when they are trying to figure out where to place you. Since each one of the decks is primarily controlled by one gang or several gangs that get along with one another, they are careful when placing new inmates on a deck. I looked at him, upset at the fact that I wouldn't be returning to my deck and said, "No," as if I had been defeated.

"Your bond is high enough that we are placing you in the 500s," he said, grabbing my arm and shoving me toward that unfamiliar part of the jail.

While I had come back to that familiar place I had learned to call home, I was entering unchartered territory that I'm not familiar with. I only hope I can make it through this… this time around.

Chapter 18

On The Way Back

o o o o o o o o o o o o o o o o o o o o o o o o o o o o o o o o o o o o o o

"Character is determined more by the lack of certain experience than by those one has had."

Friedrich Nietzsche

"Ryan?" an unfamiliar voice asked on the other end of the line.

I wondered who it could be on the phone. I had that familiar gut-wrenching feeling, reminiscent of when I passed a police officer while speeding or drunk. I guess that feeling never leaves. My Mom says she still gets that feeling when she gets a phone call in the middle of the night. It makes her wonder if something has happened to me or one of my brothers.

"Who is this?" I asked back, waiting for the explanation to come for the phone call.

"Ryan, I would like to do an article on you and how you turned your life around in military school. I was hoping to learn why you chose to come back to your hometown for your senior year." I couldn't believe it.

"An article on me?" I thought to myself . I stared off in the distance, almost feeling a change occur as I agreed to the interview and the article. The fact that I have been noticed for something positive warmed my heart as I thought about how I might finally be remembered for something good; that I had worked through my past and had come out on the other side a changed and better man. Seeing the article published in the local *Kane County Chronicle* made me feel different; a changed man embraced by the community I had been forced to leave.

Fact is, I just wanted to come back home. I wanted to end my senior year with the high school experience of going to prom and being in a normal school setting with peers and longstanding friendships.

I entered my senior year finding that time mended the wreckage that the crew and I left behind. I found myself almost alone. Most of my friends had dropped out or graduated, staying in apartments around town. I found that I was still deemed an outcast among certain crowds of people. There was a girl I fell in love with the summer before starting my senior year. She drove in the drive-thru of the fast food joint where I worked. I knew her. In fact, I had met her in the past when I nearly dated her instead of the girl who got me smoking.

With her, I was able to pull back, somewhat, from my friends. With her, I continued doing well in school, finished off with A's and B's, enjoyed prom, and stayed away from doing drugs. But my friends didn't change. They were the only people I knew. New friendships just can't be created out of thin air. I got through my senior year doing as everyone did. I partied, but without the use of drugs. Instead I did what every group and every class of people did... I drank alcohol. I would go to raves in Chicago, hang out at apartments with old friends, and socialize at house parties until I lost the ability to talk clearly. I went on romantic outings and dates with my girlfriend. Everything seemed to balance out. I even got to leave the senior year in my same old style. We spray painted the school for senior prank week, launched balloons filled with Nair hair remover on top of the freshman's heads at the bon-fire, and threw eggs at people as we drove home. It was something I saw everyone doing. I figured I could still have fun as long as my grades were in order. I knew this kind of fun would have to stop as I got older and started a career, but in moderation it seemed harmless.

Unfortunately, it wasn't so harmless for the girl crossing the road that snaked around the school and to the several parking lots that surround the school of nearly 3500 kids. As we drove around the school, I thought to myself "just another block until we are home safely." I could see the flames from the bon-fire roar in the distance as kids ran around like a pack of banshees, hoping the Nair we had launched on top of their hair would wash away. Police lights flashed and sirens wailed. Arrests were ordained for the senior pranks of that night. My heart beat like the last concussions of a drummer boy marching into war.

"Give me some eggs!" I heard my friend shout from the back seat as he rolled down the window. His body arching over the opening and protruding out of the car, he barreled an egg towards a police officer surveying the scene of the bon-fire.

"Shit!" I said looking back through the rear-view mirror at the officer running towards us with egg yolk smeared across his uniform. I hit the gas to speed up and get home. I couldn't have been going too quickly because of the winding roads that curved around the school.

"Watch it!" I heard yelled from the back. Almost instinctively, I hit the brake and skidded to a stop. I heard the bones and flesh hit the fiberglass top of the car and spread across the window. It all played in slow frame camera shots as my brain, along with everyone else's in the car took in the images through a strobe effect . Adrenaline and high doses of epinephrine pumped through the synapses of neurons so that I could think quickly and evaluate the situation.

"Damn Dawg! I hit her!" I scowled as I looked through the side mirror to see the cop coming towards us some quarter mile back.

The girl bent over and slowly walked to the side of the small road where she sat back down by her friends. "I can't stay," I thought to myself as I hit the gas to get back to the safe confines of my house.

I not only made it to safety that night, I made it through the school year. Soon I would join the rest of the class sitting on a chair in the auditorium hitting beach balls back and forth in the seats to one another. Then it was off to community college, due to my poor performance freshman year, where I would work towards a more fulfilling life.

When I reached that culmination in high school, I thought; I am different. I am a graduate. Tonight, I will sit and let earlier events wash away. I have made it back to that familiar place I call home, but I am entering unchartered territory. I am not familiar with it all. I only hope I can make it through this... this time around.

Chapter 19

High Profile Criminals

o o o o o o o o o o o o o o o o o o o o o o o o o o o o o o o

"Time is the longest distance between two points."

Tennessee Williams

"Here's your cell," the officer pointed to a cell that had just popped open. "Throw your shit in there and you can sort it all out tonight."

I looked around the 500s, a maximum security part of the jail, and noticed that it was all very different here. There were no lights to cook from since the ceilings were too high. There was no upper level or even lower level to the 500s. It was all on one even surface so the guards could look in on us more easily from their command center behind the bulletproof glass on the other side of the large barred window that made up the long wall on one side of the room. It was bigger than the other galleries, perhaps half the size of a basketball court. Instead of solid iron doors with a small opening, these cells had conventional bars making up the electric cell doors. There were also cameras mounted on the sides of the gallery so that if the officers actually cared, they could keep an eye on our every movement.

"What deck you come from, nigga?" I was asked by a small black guy who bore scars on his stomach and legs from being riddled with bullets. He looked at me intensely, checking for tattoos and sizing me up. As a small crowd gathered around to hear my answer, I walked towards my cell to create a wall between me and them, all the while sweeping the area around me with my eyes.

"I clearly might not be welcomed here." I thought to myself, looking at this guy, Rio, as he approached. His head was only half done in braided rows, the other half still stood up in an afro.

"I came from the 300s." I said vaguely. I saw him shake up with another person standing by him disrespecting another gang by throwing down three fingers, a gesture that means "love" in American Sign Language.

"I ain't shit, homie," I added, finally letting them rest on the idea of what to do with me. Still, this also meant that I am alone and without protection.

I sat down as lunch trays were delivered to the cage and passed through a small opening to the line of inmates receiving their trays. I sat down at a table with a group of Latinos, figuring that I had more in common with them since I am fairly well-versed in Spanish.

"Who's my cellie?" I asked the one sitting across from me.

"Villain," he replied.

"He here?" I asked.

"He's at court today. He ain't big on having a cellie," he stated, with a smirk on his face.

I knew I had to get off of this gallery. I am not supposed to be in the 500s. I have DUIs, not murder charges. Most of the people in the 500s are here for disciplinary reasons, or for murder and attempted murder charges. I kept my sharpened six-inch pencil close to me throughout my time on this gallery. I played out my alter ego outside and inside my cell. I said I was busted on drug charges and a manufacturing case. Luckily, I knew enough about drugs, gangs, and the right contacts from earlier in life, I could play the part. I made sure I was heard speaking Spanish to one of the Latinos so they knew that I wasn't just another white guy. I was one of them.

As Villain entered the gallery from that morning's court, I saw fingers pointed in my direction. He was tattooed and marked up with scars all over his head. He was a Latino and a gang banger from out where I stayed. He had been on this gallery for a year or two, fighting a murder charge caused when one of his guys rolled over on him for a straight eight plea agreement. In other words, he was going to get eight years straight for testifying against his friend for his role in the murders. He was young, not even old enough to have a legal drink, but he was strong. We worked out every day together with our group of Latinos. Every now and then we would get a newspaper. It was always interesting to see the face of some of the guys I was with on this gallery on the front page being indicted for murder or "9-1's" as these acts are normally referred to in a gang shooting.

I found it, at first, uncomfortable being here with this crowd of people. But, after a while you start to change. That story you tell to make it through the day becomes you. The only thing that tells you otherwise is the voice you talk to on the phone. Hell, you are one of them. For all people know, you are in there for murder. However, lies can only take you so far. What courtroom you are in, and what your paperwork says from court all tell a different story. Mentally, you lose track of who you really are. You start to wonder if that person is any longer a part of you, or whether you have been overcome with the convict mentality. Everything just becomes another day in jail carrying shanks and making allies. Only at night when everyone is asleep, and I find myself wondering about those I love, do I find some peace in this otherwise cold place. Only then do I find peace and escape from this world. Only then am I allowed to be me.

Chapter 20

College, Parties, And DUIs

o o o o o o o o o o o o o o o o o o o o o o o o o o o o o o o o o o o o o o o

"Discontent is the first necessity of progress."

Thomas A. Edison

Throughout college my drinking career skyrocketed. I was taught how to drink, puke, and drink again. Alcohol has a way of intensifying every emotion and feeling and projecting it in the worst way toward unsuspecting individuals.

It would get me in a series of close calls: near car accidents and blackouts. At Southern Illinois University I partied and lost my shoes. At University of Illinois I partied and lost my high school sweetheart. At Eastern Illinois University I partied and broke restaurant windows when a guy was thrown through a front window during a drunken brawl. It always brought an exciting, unexpected turn of events to the course of an evening. It was a staple of college and of my life. I felt alive when I was out and partying, not with drugs, but with alcohol. Alcohol gave me the ability to fly, yet in the end, it took away the sky.

Fortunately, throughout this time, I maintained my grades. I found myself in an honor society throughout college. While looking at going into premed for psychiatry, I decided to alter my plans after seeing a course in mortuary science. It was perfect for me. It was the here and now plan, rather than waiting for six or so more years to get on with life. I started working at a funeral home in town and found it to be everything I wanted. I used my medical studies embalming bodies and even my skills in art in piecing them back together after horrific accidents. I got to use psychology when helping families work through the stages of grief. Moreover, I got to help others. I felt I was leaving a positive impact by helping others through something I was very familiar with... hard times. I even was able to branch out and really come to like the business side of things. I liked working with numbers and making contacts with the community. I found the career I loved. Nevertheless, going into mortuary school, I received two DUIs within one week's time.

After the first one, I had one month to drive before the suspension kicked in. For me that meant one month to party. But, once you enter the police database, a red flag goes up anytime that you step into a car and out onto the road. All it took was for them to scan my plates and follow me for a block before they caught me slipping up on a near stop at a stop sign. Each time was the same: I would return home to my Mom, worried and upset when she wouldn't see the car. Every time I would justify myself by accusing the police of being biased against me. In some ways, I still feel that they no longer exist to help the community. They seem to have lost their old role as mentors and neighbors. They no longer suffer with their community; rather, they deliver more suffering to the community by leaning on the backbone of crime and punishment. I felt like my life came to a halt. Nobody understood how easy it was to receive a DUI.

My anger with the system didn't serve me well when I used a large rock to break out a half a dozen windows on squad cars upon being released that evening. It really didn't help in defending my case when I blew a .3 Blood Alcohol Content when the legal limit was .08 BAC. After an initial animated tone when I tried to hand the officer a five dollar bill to replace the insurance card I couldn't find, and an amused tone when I stumbled out of the car and nearly fell, his tone became very serious after he saw that number. Instead the policeman paused and looked at me as if I were in absolute desperate need of help. Then he said, "Are you aware that with this blood alcohol content you are about halfway to dying in the hospital?"

I wasn't the least bit taken aback. I was still upset at the fact that I knew I was drunk and that was the reason I had pulled off at the convenience store to fall asleep. I looked back into the multiple eyes he seemed to have and said, "I've got halfway to go then, don't I?"

I just didn't get it. My two DUI cases would be dragged out through the court system for almost two years before a judgment was set. By that time, I received my third DUI and the combination of all three sentenced me to some alcohol treatment, community service, and a victim impact panel where I heard some guy who makes more money than I would ever make tell me how he had to spend something like three months in jail for killing a kid after leaving a golf outing. Shit, who is he to complain? In my opinion, he got off easy. I just didn't get it. I wasn't there to merely

compare myself to these people; they were there with a message. I had to quit drinking. I had to re-evaluate why I drink. What was it that I was seeking? Did I not like being me? Was it an escape? What was it?

When I came home and rested my head upon my pillow, knowing that my Mom was down the hall, only then did I find peace and escape from this world. Only then was I allowed to be me.

Chapter 21

Fighting Over State Pants

o o o o o o o o o o o o o o o o o o o o o o o o o o o o o o o

"Majority rule only works if you're also considering individual rights. Because you can't have five wolves and one sheep voting on what to have for supper."

Larry Flynt

When I came on to the 500s I didn't come alone. I brought two friends with me. You see, every Sunday, inmates were provided with razors and nail clippers that had to be returned intact after using. I brought with me two friends from the 300s. One friend was a thick plastic spoon; its handle had been clipped using nail clippers. I used the floor to file down the edges and wrapped torn linen and shirts around the spoon for a handle. The other trusted friend I had was my seven-inch sharpened pencil that I kept unused. I had jammed the eraser end into a chess piece and wrapped it up in a torn t-shirt. I kept these hidden within my bedroll while forced to be in the company of others during the 14 hours locked outside of my cell. The day these friends would become important came soon enough.

Hold up a minute," I said to the guys I was playing cards with. One of the things you learn on decks is to never "snooze" on where everybody is and what is going on around you, especially in the 500s.

"What you doin, dawg?" my partner asked me as I stood up from the card table.

"That nigga's wearing my pants," I answered, amazed that Rio had the nerve to steal the pants I put in the laundry. I thought I left them back in the 300s, but here they were. He was sitting on top of the table playing cards with three others who were of no concern to me. I wasn't sure how I was going to go about it, but I guess I assumed that if I put him out there as a thief or confronted him sounding as though it were possibly a mistake, I would get my pants back. Either way, I was going to get my pants back.

"Those are my pants you're wearing." I knew he heard me because he put his head down and looked at the pants he was wearing and glared at the people he was playing cards with at the table. His cellie and fellow gang member sat on the other side. At this point, I had forced a confrontation. I wasn't going to go on not holding my head up and appear as some easy mark for others.

"You gonna give up those pants?" I asked him, half nervous about where this might lead, and half pissed off that this bullet-riddled fool wanted to square off over some state pants. Even he knew that it wasn't just about the pants anymore. It was about respect.

"You gonna steal another man's pants just like that?" I was hoping for an answer, an action. I questioned hitting him, or "stealing on him" right then and there, hoping that a well-landed blow would give me the time to square off with his cellie. Fact is, I had two of these fools to worry about. I had to get back to my cell if they paired up. I would have to get to my shanks.

"I didn't steal them, I took them!" he said, still sitting down but looking at me in anticipation. I didn't do anything. I just looked at him and turned the matter over in my head trying to figure out a way that this wouldn't resort to a fight and going to segregation. I had to keep face. I couldn't be like that white kid in the 300s. I'll kill a guy before I get treated that way. I walked about twenty feet away from the table, stopped, and walked back to him. I knew what I had to do.

I stood behind him again and asked simply, "You gonna give them up or what?"

"You ain't getting them back. These are my pants" he said. Rio stood up and removed his shirt, showing off some tattoos over his scrawny body. His stomach was mangled and pieced back together with a scar that rode up the center where the hospital ripped him open to retrieve the bullets that had once been buried inside him. I stood ready and displayed my hands in front of my face. This was how it had to be. I looked at his shoulders to watch for any quick movement I could act on. Before I took the liberty of snatching the life away from him, I asked him one last question, "Why?"

That question circled my own head time and time again. Why would he take my pants? Why has he got something to prove? Why can't he just do his time here? Why didn't he just give them up? Why?

I swept to the side of him, anxious for the blows to start. I questioned delivering a hard right, but momentum ceased. Everything was slow. I felt sluggish. Nothing was happening. I waited for his quick jab to come. He stood there prepared.

"Break it up man. It's just some ugly pants," a big black, older man said, stepping between us.

"Let him go!" Rio demanded, still appearing tough. The Latinos congregated under the television that was mounted high up on the wall to the side of us. They had taken bets that Rio was going to get pounded on.

"What? You gonna get them pants for me?" I asked, as if there was a glimmer of hope that he could provide reason to this situation.

"No," he stated, as if the whole thing should be chalked up to a loss.

"Well, I gotta do what I gotta do then." I said, with a shrug of my shoulders.

As I rolled my eyes I caught a glimpse of a figure moving towards me. I turned my head to see a light-skinned, small, black guy named Wimp moving closely towards me with his gold teeth glinting through his pursed lips.

"Shit!" I thought to myself as I realized that my cell door where the shanks are hidden is now past him. I sidestepped quickly so that both Wimp and Rio were within my vision's perimeter. I backed up to a cell door to the side view of the camera and stood prepared.

"What you gonna do then, nigga?" Wimp asked as he bounced and stepped around looking as though he were going into a golden glove boxing match. I knew I could get one of them and maybe even a blow or two on the other, but my two fists were no match for the four that would be swung from my left and right sides.

"Meds!" I heard the officer yell as the front door behind the cage popped open. We all quickly dropped our hands and dispersed. I could hear my foes talking. They were saying how I was a coward and other things that would draw one to immediate punches had it not been for the guard. So, with the guard there, I saw this as my opportunity at redemption by sticking up for myself. The incident would be squashed quickly by the guard before I was caught up in a beating.

"I am not the one who needs some protection! You need another nigga to help you out with your troubles!" I yelled, making the guard partially aware, though his eyes and actions never changed at all during the course of my yelling. When the officer left the deck and locked the door behind him, we all looked at one another. Next thing we knew, we got some shit for talking in midst of the guard's appearance.

"Everyone in their damn rat-holes! This is a shakedown!" I heard. The next minute guards were flooding the deck and suited up for battle. We all returned to our cells, convinced this was about the fight. As we entered the cells, I quickly pulled my property inside the barred cell door and hid the shanks, slipping them inside a tear in my plastic mattress and shoving them deep inside.

"Take these hot pants back, fool." I heard Rio say from the cell next door as he stuck his hands out through the bars of his cell door and reached around to my cell. "Don't say shit, nigga," he added as I took the pants from him.

"I ain't like that man," I stated confidently.

It was a bogus shakedown. They found a couple things but nothing too major. They asked questions of each inmate. They asked if there were any problems or anything they would like to share with them. They ask, knowing it would be certain death if anyone ever leaked information to the cops. Plus, you are putting your trust in the same people that want you locked up and are gunning for the day they get to work you over. These guys are no better than the cops that put you in this place. You have no true friends in this place.

As we were released from our cells, Wimp came immediately over to my cell. I sat, waiting for them to come, with one of the shanks hidden by my side.

"Hey dawg, I didn't know them were your pants. We thought you was on some gangbangin' shit and that's why I stepped in. We all cool now?" he said as a message of truce and acceptance that I stood my ground.

"We straight man," I said. I simply wanted to just blow the anxiety and stress away.

Just another day behind bars. I work to cope with this new life. Like a patient who has a cancerous tumor that the doctor removes, along with parts of the kidney and intestines, so that he will not be in pain as the cancer grows within him, I too remove parts of myself to let this new me take over. I remove my heart and numb myself to the life I left behind. I take away my brain, my way of thinking, the hope I had some time ago. Instead, I retrain myself. There is no compassion for a guy like me in this world. There is no sense of relief; only quiet desperation.

Chapter 22

Overdose

o o o o o o o o o o o o o o o o o o o o o o o o o o o o o o

"Your vision will become clear only when you can look into your own heart. Who looks outside, dreams; who looks inside, awakes."

Carl Jung

I still pursued Mortuary College. Despite the DUIs, I received my license in six months. It only took me a few days more to lose it again when I was caught attempting to pull a u-turn on the interstate after passing up the exit I needed and driving down the shoulder of the road to catch the break in the median of the interstate where I could turn around. Oddly enough, on that same night I had been pulled over and released after the officer deemed me sober. I feared having to call my Mom, tell her that I had received my third DUI, and that her car was impounded. Beyond that, I feared what this would do to me. My Mom asked me to take it easy. I couldn't even do that right. Why can't I ever get a break? The police offered to give me a ride. Instead, when I got in the cruiser, I was simply dropped off just outside of Cook County and left to walk the thirty miles back home; a feat that a marathon runner would have trouble walking, nevertheless a drunken college student. I was upset that I was arrested, upset with the police, and pissed off that this would ruin my life. I was tired and drunk.

"How the hell am I gonna get home!" I yelled out and cursed the police officer for leaving me in front of a hotel when I had no money and no identification.

So, in the brilliance of my drunken escapade, I threw a rock at a hotel window while attempting to get inside and simply get some sleep. Crash!

The outermost sliding door broke and shattered throughout the porch, leaving me still unable to get inside.

"What was that?" I asked myself as I heard some noise down the way. It was one of the hotel employees. She was heading home.

"Lay down behind the porch." I told myself, peering out into the parking lot through the one-foot gap between the concrete and the three-foot tall, thick, wooden railing.

"Shit, she's looking right at me and calling someone! Run!" I said to myself as I grabbed a piece of glass and dashed across the parking lot and into a cemetery next door. There I sat behind a bush and kept an eye on the hotel. I looked down at the ground and the graves littering the cemetery.

"Why can't I live a fulfilling life? What is the matter with me? I can't ever get out of this one. I can't put my Mom through what I have done. It's over for me; I can't live with this disappointment." Tears trickled down my face and the salt from the tears tasted bitter against my trembling lips as I stroked my wrist with the broken piece of glass. The tears stopped and I felt at peace with each cut. I fell into the abyss of drunken depression. I had fallen for the dream of a perfect life, but instead I fell apart. My eyes closed and I fell asleep. I was awakened by a police officer tapping my shoulder and a bright light illuminating the darkness that consumes the cemeteries during the long nights. In the end, it was my Mom who comforted me. But it was also my Mom who hurt me more than the deepest cut inflicted by that shard of broken glass. It was my heart that broke when I saw the tears from my Mom as she stood at the front of the police station, feeling helpless and completely aware of what was wrong with me.

My license was stripped away once again, but this time it would be some three to five years to get it back. I was about four months into mortuary school and had not made anything lower than a B; I had almost all As. I had no idea how I was going to make it through the last eight months of college without the ability to commute to and from the campus. Plus, I had to quit my job at the funeral home where I had been working due to my inability to drive. Everything in life was halted. But I had to keep going; I was so close to my dream.

"Why don't you come out and live in my place? I have two extra bedrooms in a huge apartment in the city. You'll love it out there," I was asked by one of the students in my class who was in his mid to late thirties, wore long hair and looked like he never took a shower in his lifetime. He drove an older Cadillac that was beaten up and never washed inside or out. Sometimes he would bring his dog with him to school. Many times he would leave prior to the day being over. His blue eyes were often overcast and half-closed. His nose was long and narrow. He would often talk of his hippie days touring with the Grateful Dead. I had no choice. And, to be honest, I jumped at the rent free opportunity and the ride to college. I never questioned my decision. Often, when he left early, I would be stranded. Sometimes I could catch rides. Sometimes I would stay at a girl's apartment close to the school. Other times I would hop a ride with a guy who would become a good drinking buddy. He even let me get some work in at his family's funeral home. I never questioned it more than when I left early with him and went down to the near west side of Chicago. The place we visited was a neighborhood where cops pulled you over if you were white and touring the neighborhood because you didn't belong. I can't imagine the psychological effects that has on the community, or the message it sends to the young kids there. I didn't want to be there. I definitely didn't want to go to the corner to score some heroin.

Every street we turned down we would hear the kids shout out, "Rocks! Blows!" The words corresponding to crack and heroin would prompt a line of traffic. Other members of the crew positioned down the block would alert the young kid handling the dope if there was a cop rolling through the area.

I didn't like the mess I got myself into, but I wanted to finish college. My desire to succeed would drive me to great lengths. It would even lead me to grab a friend's ankles after he overdosed so that I could carry him out the back door and into the alley. My drinking never took a day's break. He kept a leash on me through the money his dad would send him each day. That income kept up his one hundred and fifty dollar a day habit. Not included in that was the twenty to thirty dollars he would spend per day so that I could maintain my personal drinking career.

However, my college career was not worth the evening I spent consuming alcohol and led to my curiosity of what these new drugs would feel like. I bent down to the mahogany dining room table and sucked in the powder that was neatly divided into lines. A feeling like I was weightless came over me. It was as if I was lightheaded; hell, perhaps I was, because the next thing I knew was I was sitting in the shower in only my boxers while cold water ran over my face as my roommate stayed bent over, staring at me and trying to bring me back to life. After the early evening spent coughing blood and struggling to gasp for air, I found myself handcuffed to a hospital bed because I had missed my court date. I just wanted to go home. I was tired and depleted. After everything was done and bail was posted for me so that I could walk out of that hospital a changed man, I would find that there is no compassion for a guy like me in this world. No sense of relief; only quiet desperation.

Chapter 23

Sentencing

o o o o o o o o o o o o o o o o o o o o o o o o o o o o o o o o o o o

"Tact is the art of making a point without making an enemy."

Isaac Newton

At Kane County Jail we created activities that would keep us entertained for a while on the deck. We played games of handball against one of the walls, hitting a ball made up of tightly tied socks and t-shirts. We played in card tournaments, made dice out of molded toilet paper, played football off of the stainless steel table tops using a folded piece of paper in the shape of a triangle, trying to flick it across the table until a piece of the football scored when it hung off the opposite end of the table. Most of the days, I sat drawing portraits for others on the deck, watched some television, and once or twice a week I would place a call to talk with my Mom or Dad.

I was tired of this place and the drama that seemed to arise weekly. There was always a fight, gangs at war, or another brilliant idea from the sheriff of mixing the decks with different gangs so that gang rivals could learn to co-exist with one another on the decks. I just wanted to get out. Commissary was expensive… too expensive. Plus, I was tired of seeing those I loved through the bulletproof glass in the visiting room. I missed seeing the sun and the freedom of just being outside. I needed a change. I needed to get out of this place.

"Step out for court!" the officer yelled out on the deck. I stepped to the door and then waited inside the cage shoulder to shoulder with the other inmates from my gallery, watching inmates from other galleries being marched out one by one and shackled from their feet to their wrists, bound for that day's court appearance.

Clack! The iron door with the bulletproof glass leading to the long silent corridors opened. It was the only time I was able to see the outside, through two windows that sat along the walk to the command center that watches over the flow going in and out of visits and those going to and from court. Deck by deck, gallery by gallery, wing by wing, we were marched into the same elevator that took us up to the main level of the jail and back down to the lower level I had come in from some six months earlier. We were escorted from command center to command center and told to wait until the next group was ready. Finally, we felt a breeze of real unfiltered natural air coming through the last door as we were loaded into that large white van and hauled off to court.

For six months I had counted down time by a mere set of court dates. But this day was different. I would sign my papers today, leading me to finally accept and come to terms with the things I had done. As I was unloaded from the van into the back garage door of the court house I had hoped to never enter again, I thought of nothing except leaving for the unknown world of prison. I had heard little bits and pieces of what was to come. However, I had learned truth is hard to find in jail. You're never sure that the information you get is accurate. Most of the time, it is half-truths. I just wanted out of jail.

I was tired of being crammed into the courtroom holding cells that consisted of two rooms each with a cement bench only big enough to hold three or four of the ten or more inmates going to court that day. Beyond that, the room was a 6 x 10 foot cell with a small waist high cement division and behind it sat a stainless steel toilet/sink combo. I was sick of being crammed into these rooms like it was a concert and we were all awaiting our turn to get center stage. A camera looked over the "bull-pens" we waited in. We would perk up every time the bailiff opened the door ready to call out a name, opening the door and letting in a little air into the enclosed space. There were no openings into these cells except for where the bagged lunches of an orange, two stale cookies, a juice carton, and warm bologna sandwich arrived.

"It's my lawyer!" I almost screamed aloud as he entered through the door and pulled me out of the bull-pen to a similar room just across from it where the other inmates would stare across through the bulletproof glass that lined the wall of the bull-pen and see what it was that was going on with your case, making sure that you were not leaking any information. Inside of this cell, sometimes used as a temporary holding cell handling the overflow of inmates, was the stainless steel table where I sat staring at the documents laid on the table in front of me. It was my plea. All I had to do was write my name on the blank line and seal my fate away to the care of Illinois Department of Corrections.

"Okay," I said, signing the piece of paper. It indicated that I would not take a felony for the theft from the funeral home, so it wouldn't hinder future careers or job decisions. However, I would receive three felony convictions for three DUIs. One would be dropped as part of the deal. The three felonies would carry sentences of three, three, and two years, totaling eight years.

"It's over," I thought to myself as I left the room to confront the judge. I was just relieved it was all over. There I stood, mad again at the world, or at least the state's attorneys and judges for this ridiculous sentence for DUI charges when I could get a similar amount of time for armed robbery, attempted murder, or second degree murder. I guess it might be true; it is always the victims that get screwed. In my case, I am my own victim. I couldn't believe that others couldn't see that I had a career. I was more used to working and earning an honest living than taking their money and further lining the pockets of the corrupt officials running the penitentiaries and government throughout Illinois. Hell, this is the only state that continually makes the news for its corrupt politicians; politicians who later ask for leniency and early release from the penitentiary. No offense, but screw them and the horse they rode in on! They are no better than I or the thousands of others who can't be heard because, as Benjamin Franklin once said, "There is no room for compassion in law."

"This will forever change your life, Ryan. I only hope that it is for the better," the judge said. I rolled my eyes and wanted to strangle his smug ass for thinking he can sit up on his damn pedestal and play God with people's lives.

My first stay in jail, and now I was going to the penitentiary. I never thought I would become this man. I wish I could have done so much differently. That is just it. I wish for the past and pray that tomorrow will bring hope.

Chapter 24

For Better Or Worse

o o o o o o o o o o o o o o o o o o o o o o o o o o o o o o o o o o o o o

"He who opens a school door, closes a prison."

Victor Hugo

I joined back up with another class in Worsham Mortuary College almost three months later. This time I would stay at home and find ways of getting to and from school. It was a month or so into school when I saw her. Her name was Allena, and her golden blond hair gleamed against her blue eyes. She carried herself with a sense of pride, like there wasn't a worry in the world. She was beautiful and I wanted her to be mine. I would catch myself watching as her petite, athletic body trailed the hallways back and forth to classes. It was as if I were a moth attracted to the flame. I couldn't draw my attention away from her.

As I got to know more about her, I was blinded to the negatives that may have existed. All I saw was that she didn't use drugs, didn't drink, made good grades, and wanted the same things in life I wanted. When I was with her, the courts and all my problems didn't matter. I was afraid to tell her the extent of my problems in fear that she would not be with me. I went on a couple adventures while I was with her early on. One night I took a couple of pills of ecstasy and confessed my undying love to her in the strip club where she worked. For the most part, though, I was reserved. I would look forward to tomorrow and when I would get to see her again. Not another female in the world, aside from my Mom, seemed to matter. We were determined that all we needed in life was each other. We both graduated from Mortuary College making exceptionally good grades, and more and more I thought my dreams were obtainable.

My dreams now had someone in them with me. I could picture a family with her. She stopped working at the strip club shortly after graduation. Weeks after, we took a vacation to Mexico together. On January 1st while celebrating New Year's Eve at a nice hotel and restaurant, I took the leap of faith and asked her into my life, or the life I chose to share with her. July 2nd, we vowed to be together for better or worse. We slipped the covenant of marriage over one another's finger, solidifying the love we felt.

However, our marriage would be mostly for worse when I received another DUI the night of my bachelor party. I even had to run off of the altar the afternoon of our rehearsal to puke outside. I didn't tell her about the DUI until after our marriage, and even then, I hid the fact that another DUI could mean prison time. I was afraid to let her completely in on my problems since she always said that the only reason she would ever divorce me would be because of prison.

I found new ways to move forward and carry on. I had accomplished my greatest dream. My marriage created moments I have never been more proud of in my adult life. No drug or alcohol could strip those accomplishments and memories from me. But as the justice system closed in on me, the memory of those accomplishments would bring me an unbearable pain and heartache that I don't think I can ever forget. There were many nights I would be withdrawn and contemplative as to what my next move would be. As I think back to those times, I wish I could have done so much differently. Yet, that is just it; I wish for the past and pray that tomorrow will bring me hope.

Part 2

Chapter 25

Stateville Recieving

o o o o o o o o o o o o o o o o o o o o o o o o o o o o o o o o o o o o o o o

"But the thing I felt most strongly about, and put at the end of one of the prison diaries, was education."

Jeffery Archer

Pulling into the prison system's receiving dock for the entire mid and northern Illinois was nothing like going into jail. It really hit home. There is no going back. There is no escape. You are stuck in this situation and no screams or cries will do anything for you except land you in an isolated protective custody cell. It brought to mind the stuff that makes up movies and nightmares. We sat that thirty or forty minute drive in almost complete silence.

We pulled up along a structure that would take up six football stadiums, double-fenced, with rolls of barbed wire running along the entire length top to bottom. Large towers were housed with men operating the spotlights and holding the rifles that took careful aim at the van as we approached. In front of us, coming straight at us, were two armed guards with dogs checking in their new shipment of fresh meat. After searching the vehicle and thoroughly scanning every inch with mirrors and drug dogs, they waved their hands and spoke into a walkie-talkie attached to their shoulders. Next thing we knew, the gates of hell opened up and we pulled between two extremely tall electric fences.

"Gentlemen! Cooperate with me and we will get through this quickly and you'll be in your home for the next thirty days or so before you know it. In other words, shut the hell up!" the prison guard yelled, arranging the list in front of him with each of our offenses and pictures.

He called us off individually, and when he was done he turned around with a half smirk and said, "Welcome to Stateville Penitentiary receiving area for the entire mid and northern Illinois."

With that, he was gone and the next gate opened up to bring us home. What we walked into next was beyond imagination. It was a large gym the size of an entire football stadium divided into three sections. As we walked, shackled from hand to foot, we were led into one of four large caged-in sections. In each section there were rows of steel benches. In front was a toilet almost completely open for all to see. On the far side of this large cage, on the opposite side of the gym, was another cage which was as big as all three of these smaller cages. In hand was the property that I was allowed to take with me: ten photos, one Bible, and ten "write-outs" or stamped envelopes. Nothing else would travel with me except for the clothes I would be wearing for a little longer.

Van after van and bus after bus from other counties flooded in and filled the entire gym. The guards shuffled us out of this section one county at a time. Our property was checked in by a guard who was up front behind a folding card table. Then we were led into the other section. It consisted of an elaborate display of catwalks where armed guards patrolled back and forth, itching for the moment one of us would get out of hand while being hassled and humiliated by the two guards who watched us strip down, tossing aside the orange jumpsuit we wore. Lined up against the wall as if facing a firing squad, we were ordered through the same routine of bending over and lifting our feet up as they checked us over and shot remarks about penis size, physical fitness or ethnic origin. Then, to kill the parasites and microorganisms that thrive in the county jail, we were ordered to shower thoroughly with the soap they provided, throwing it at our feet. We were dogs, animals, treated as if we were pure garbage and a waste of flesh. Each one of use would be ridiculed by the day's end in some fashion, deflating any glimmer of hope that there was one decent guard amongst the wolves. They were all the same, taking their shots while pushing you along the line. We walked out of the shower and lined up as naked as the day we were brought into this world, reborn again, except this time as a convict. We were given a light blue shirt, blue pants, and undergarments courtesy of inmates serving time at Centralia Penitentiary in Illinois.

We walked through a never-ending maze of temporary partitions and walls leading us from one cubicle to the next registering our blood, medical information, dental work, mug shots, fingerprints, psychological profile, and every scrap and ounce of personal information into the federal and state databases. We did this until we were finished some six or

seven hours later. Then we were released back to the other section within the large fenced cage. Finally we were seated. Exhausted from the barrage of attacks and physical pain of the whole ordeal, we were given that same sack lunch consisting of green bologna on white bread.

Eventually, at what time I could only guess, the sun went down and the birds stopped chirping. Then, and only then, did we see the final and third section of this stadium. There were multiple galleries consisting of three levels each with twenty cells and two showers at the far end. There were no windows, no clocks, and no source of entertainment except your religious book, old letters, and pictures. We would stay here for a month until we were deemed properly placed within the Illinois penal system.

Over a period of a month, the mind can get creative as to what one might do for fun. My cellie had somehow managed to sneak a black pen past the guards and gave it to me so I could write letters and poetry. Each breakfast, lunch, and dinner we were fed meals on styrofoam trays. I had carefully broken a hole through the lid of my tray and, using wet toilet paper, fastened it to the wall so I could shoot hoops in my cell between doing sets of dips on the steel bunk bed and pushups off of the toilet seat. Along with each meal we were given milk and juice cartons. We tore off the four sides of each carton after every meal and drew a card number and suit until we had a full deck of cards.

Those nights were as long as the days. I would toss and turn, my bones aching on the steel bed with the half-inch thick mattress. I recalled a different life. A life I would play over and over in my head. I remembered the not so good days prior to my divorce when I lied to Allena and to our minister about being drunk. I remembered the camping trip that led to her leaving me after I woke up in a hospital from going on an all-night binger with drugs and alcohol. Everything I did to just escape the pain of knowing this day was coming had come to naught. Now, all I wanted to do was go back and recreate differences in those moments. Now, I just wished I knew where I was going in life.

Chapter 26

Sheridan Correctional Center

o o o o o o o o o o o o o o o o o o o o o o o o o o o o o o o

"One of the many lessons that one learns in prison is, that things are what they are and what they will be."

Oscar Wilde

It was only two weeks before I was going home and I didn't even know it. I had finally arrived at the joint I always hoped I would go to... Sheridan Correctional Center. This is a rehabilitation facility for those suffering from drug and alcohol addictions. I prayed that in the year I left, I would perhaps get over my desire to ruin everything still good in my life. Only problem is, I didn't know who I was or who I wanted to be anymore. Part of me just wanted to come here for the "good time" that the state knocked off of your sentence, accrediting you an additional forty-five days for every ninety days served.

I immediately cliqued up with a Latino from my area, and we would Live out our mornings going to chow and participating in group meeting where I would withdraw and hide that part of myself I had lied about for so long. Here at Sheridan we held two or three meeting each day. We had to hold hands and pray, followed by a song. I would roll my eyes at the inmates ingrained to the guard's mentality of "tricking" or telling on other inmates. I knew time here would have to be played out and pretended to be someone I wasn't sure I wanted to be.

For two weeks I spent time locked up in another cell, waiting for the next yard time or opportunity to use the telephone. For two weeks I spent time watching television in my cell and thinking about the culinary arts class I wanted to get into. For two weeks I spent time thinking about how my last year of incarceration would be played out at former governor Rod

Blagoavich's project penitentiary built to provide inmates a foundation to start a new life. Illinois' former governor who will, possibly, soon hold himself to no better standard than those already serving time inside of what, I bet, is some sweet minimum security penitentiary with carpet in the cell. Maybe he will sleep next to our former Secretary of State, George Ryan, who is also serving time.

After those two weeks, I was called over to the head counselor's office. The office took up a corner cell. All the furniture had been removed, and it was wired up for internet connection and had other amenities. I sat on the formed concrete bench along side the stairs leading to the upper gallery awaiting my turn, waiting to see why the counselor had sent for me.

"Harnish, have a seat," the counselor said, waving his hand toward the chair which sat along the wall just in front of his desk. He never came on to our deck like the others who ran our groups; those who wore nicer clothes and smelled like a freshly-smoked cigarette. This guy wore a tight t-shirt, accentuating his big arms and chest. He never really talked to us except for our initial meeting the day we arrived.

"What the hell am I doing here?" I thought to myself as I saw him typing on the computer next to him.

"Is this about the good time from the construction class in Hardin County Work Camp I was supposed to get?" I asked him, wondering whether they wouldn't be honoring the contract since they shipped me here two days before the contract was to be done.

"I finished all the work for that contract. I was just waiting for the few days remaining on the contract time to come up but then they transferred me here. Hell, at that point I didn't even want to come here. I could have finished my time up there and still be out in September of 2009." I waited his response as my blood boiled, waiting for the bad news to come regarding my contract.

"Don't worry about your contract. You're going home Tuesday. I have you on immediate release." he said, looking me dead in the eyes. I didn't know what to say. I didn't want to say he was wrong and miss my opportunity to leave. Hell, I have a year left. I just sat there, unsure what to do or say.

"There's no frigging way I am going home." I thought to myself.

The counselor must have known what I was thinking. He just looked at me and finally said, after what felt like hours, "I caught an error the state made on your calculation sheet. One of your cases was supposed to be concurrent, making it five years instead of eight you were to be sentenced."

I didn't know what to say. I was thrilled. But then the thrill left. I was mad at the fact that a mistake had been made; a big mistake. "When was

I supposed to be out?" I asked him, knowing that I had been held past the out-date of my sentence.

"About now," he stated, as if this were a mere formality. "About now!" I repeated back to him loudly. I had already done the calculations in my head. I should have been out three months and ten days ago. I was wrongly held for one hundred days, not including the contract I was still waiting for from Hardin County which would give me an additional thirty days off my sentence. Hell, within that period of time my younger brother left for South Korea, Allena's grandmother died, and my grandma died. This is time they can't give back to me. Time I have spent grieving alone in the confines of my room, knowing that if I shared it with the counselor, I might get put in an isolation unit on suicide watch.

"Do you have someone that you want me to contact to pick you up? I have you paroling to your mother's house," he said, cutting off what would have been a rampage coming from my mouth.

I went calm. "My Mom," I thought to myself. I want my mother.

I looked at him and said softly, "My Mom will pick me up." "Okay, you'll be outside first thing Tuesday morning," and he ended the conversation, offering me his hand.

As I left his office something else came over me. I had written down many plans and ideas about what I would do when I got out. I heard on the news that they were taking felons into the military. I thought about leaving the country in hopes of a new and better life. I even wrote an entire business plan in hopes I might be able to open my own company within the mortuary field. I thought of some words the counselor said in group one day, "If you are true to yourself and really want to change, you will be scared the day you walk out of here." I was scared. The feeling overwhelmed me.

"I haven't learned anything yet," I thought to myself. Conflicting emotions and feelings came over me as I said to myself, "I don't want to leave."

I thought of the wreckage I had left behind and the times I was arrested. I thought of the things I would like to do and see. Now, all I wanted to do was go back and recreate differences in those moments. Now, I just wished I knew where I was going in life.

Chapter 27

Hope + Expectations = Hell

o o o o o o o o o o o o o o o o o o o o o o o o o o o o o o o o o o o

"In prison, those things withheld from and denied to the prisoner become precisely what he wants most of all."

Eldridge Cleaver

"Mail!" I heard echoed throughout the white-bricked walls I had been staring at for the past month. I couldn't wait to get out of this place. The lack of movement and stimulation caused by being locked up in these cells all day long brings to light just what my psychology professor once talked about when we were studying sensory deprivation. Everything went numb. The absence of almost all stimulation has made me volatile, irritable, and discontent. My next door neighbors flooded their cell by breaking the sprinkler nozzle located on the ceiling just so they could get out of their cell and, for a brief moment, experience a heightened sense of stimulation. I observed for hours the cold water easing it's way into my cell, and watched some twenty minutes later when the guards took them out of their cell and moved them to a place I am sure is no better than the cell they were in. Yet, as I watched the water spread over the gallery against the constant mopping efforts of some of the inmates, I wondered if I would ever see my way outside of this cell.

As I lay there on my steel bed, I stared out the front window of my cell and waited for signs of life as the guard walked the gallery handing out the mail. My body ached, my head hurt from the state of quasi-consciousness I had been living in. It is that manner of living through sleep and snapshots of dreams only to be awakened in a state of sheer boredom and disbelief, hoping that everything will someday end as a bad dream.

My days of incarceration are lived out like, I would imagine, a lonely old cancer patient confined to bed inside a hospital might exist. There the patient rests day in and day out. No family, no friends, nothing but the echoes of those around him. He holds the hope that someday he will leave this place, still an old man and with this cancer eating away at his life, but out of confinement. Inside that room, the patient gets news that his kidney and parts of his intestine must be removed to inhibit the cancer spreading into the organs listed as the tripod of life: heart, lungs, and brain. He looks around at the sterile and lonely environment that has become his home, and realizes that everything important in life that one normally holds so dear is not in this room with him. He is like any other patient in this hospital; but for him, There is no family or loved one at his side. He will ultimately die, having learned that great fact too late in life. I feel as though the patient I have described is the only man that may be able to closely portray the life we live here in Stateville Penitentiary.

I have this setting I cannot escape, almost bed ridden. I feel infected, and my insides are twisted and coiled. I can only try to remove parts of myself so that it doesn't contaminate the rest of me and drive me to the brink of insanity. I remove my heart so that I can't feel anymore. I remove my brain so that thoughts of hopelessness and abandonment will be my daily reprieve. I do all of this knowing that the one thing that is important to me now is out there and out of reach. My family is the gift I have always had, but I blew it apart early in my life. I am now that old man, dying and awaiting a day when either death or freedom will come. The only difference is that I still have more of this non-essential life to live, and my doctor is some guy who's treatment plan revolves around abusive language and a more stand-off approach; a man who wears his badge and "crap-tastic" uniform thinking that those little differences make him superior and unlike those of us on the other side of the steel doors and bulletproof glass. Problem is, these guys, like the doctor for the elderly man dying of cancer, are probably more out of touch with what is important in life than those of us suffering. I just need a change; a fresh start.

"Harnish!" I heard called out, slightly muffled by the echo produced by the large gallery and the steel and glass that separates us. I turned to see the white paper shoved through the tray port in the bulletproof glass. I jumped down from bunk welded to the white latex paint-covered brick wall and grasped the paper in my hand thinking to myself, "This is it. These are the transfer papers I have waited for a month to get."

I unfolded the piece of paper to reveal the truth that lay within. K-19, it read on the top marked in red pen. My bus leaves today. I am

sure this will be a much better place with more to offer than three small meals a day and a cell. I guessed that penitentiary code K-19 was the code for Sheridan treatment center. I had signed up to go there for alcohol treatment. It would be close to home so I would be able to see my son and my family.

As I waited for the next three hours to pass before I was to see the outside of my cell and the beginning of what will be my new life, I listened to the others call out on the gallery about where they were going based on the codes. Then I heard it. Called out amongst the gallery I heard some other inmate call out to another, "K-19! Where that is, dawg?"

I listened intently to the answer that was shouted back from the lower gallery.

"Who that is with K-19?" I heard the man answer back. I felt betrayed when the answer came.

I felt as though I had been cheated when I heard the reply, "Hey nigga, you going to Shawnee, dawg. You going to the south nigga. That shit is like Kentucky. You messed up, dawg. That joint is fucked up. They like twenty-one and three fool."

Twenty-one and three indicated the time you get outside of your cell for weightlifting, cards, gym, phone usage, and other activities that take place on the deck. In other words, an inmate is locked up for twenty-one hours out of the day and three hours are spent outside of the cell.

As I sat back, I was confused. I didn't understand why I was going to such a high security penitentiary for DUI convictions. I don't see how I belonged in a medium-maximum security penitentiary. On the other hand, I just wanted out of this cell. Since I had spent my time prior to coming to Stateville inside segregation at Kane County's illustrious jail, I hadn't talked to loved ones for over a month. I wanted to call home. No matter what mistakes were made, bottom line, I am just happy to be leaving.

Chapter 28

Leaving The Penitentiary

o o o o o o o o o o o o o o o o o o o o o o o o o o o o o o o o o

"To forgive is to set a prisoner free and discover that the prisoner was you."

Lewis B. Smedes

As I settled into my setting here at Sheridan Correctional Center, I had sowed some roots already. I came in and made a friend with whom I shared mutual acquaintances from Elgin. He was an Insane Deuce and he made some introductions when I came in on the deck. I met various other Latin Folks from around the Chicagoland area and two other Deuces that were within general population at Sheridan Correctional Center.

It was different here than at the previous penitentiaries. Gangbanging was more low-key. It wasn't out in the open like at other places. But I felt that now that I am leaving, it was time to pay respect to those with whom I was closest.

I left behind my television, electronics, food, clothing, and everything I could to those I knew. Those last couple of nights awaiting the arrival of October 28th, 2008, I lay back and thought of everything I went through. I thought of what I would do when I saw the outside. I thought of everything: my escape from this life, my son and things I wanted to do with him, my future and what my career options might be, all the way down to what I would like to eat when I got out. I had imagined this day coming. I didn't think it would be until sometime in August or September of 2009, but I imagined myself walking out those front gates a free man and shaking hands with the guards on the way out. I imagined it as it was portrayed in the movie *Shawshank Redemption*.

It was early the morning of October 28th, 2008; my cell door popped open just after breakfast. I sat and stared at it while trying to find my friend from Elgin across the crowd. I left my cell saying goodbye to my cellie. I had shared this cell with him for the two weeks I spent here at the rehabilitation program I never got into. I took a last look at the cell I was so used to and felt the tension build in my body as uncertainty and excitement grew within me. I strapped my boots to my feet and picked up the few items I would be taking with me:

* one Bible filled with folded back pages of scriptures I enjoyed. Written inside were addresses and telephone numbers I accumulated over my time,
* several pictures I had accumulated while serving time inside the penitentiary of those whose time had progressed forward as mine had stood still,
* one set of paint brushes I have had since Shawnee Correctional Center for a painting I was suppose to do for my father but there was never any paint to accompany the brushes,
* various letters I had kept from my days of waiting for the guard to deliver the anticipated words of loved ones by tossing the envelope onto my bed, and the writings I have documented while serving time… while inside and on the outs.

I walked the stretch of sidewalk, talking to the guards everyone perceived as assholes, seeing them in a different light. They were kind and considerate. They shared a part of themselves they kept hidden from a majority of the inmate population because in doing so it would make them look "soft". They explained how a cold, hard line had to be drawn to protect themselves from the inmates. At Hardin County, even at Shawnee, some of the guards did favors for the inmates, so I knew exactly what they were talking about.

I walked that sidewalk past the academic building where I hoped to attend some classes in culinary arts. I walked past the chow hall where I was to be doing my one month of cleaning pots and pans that was mandatory for inmates. I walked over to clothing where I was given the clothes I would be going home in:

* black state boots with the padding ripped out down to the sole of the boot,
* white boxers,
* white t-shirt,
* black nylon jacket,
* black dress pants,

* and white socks, all made and provided by hard-working inmates throughout the factories at Illinois State Penitentiaries.

From there, I followed the other six or so inmates going home that day, up to the office building of Sheridan to sign our final parole papers. It was one of the most memorable days of our life. I signed a blank piece of paper indicating my parole plans once released. Due to the state's mistake and the unexpected release, I had no parole conditions, no mandatory treatment, anger management, or objectives that had to be completed. My only plans were to remain in contact with my parole officer, Deb, upon release. I was given a set of restrictions. I can no longer own or carry a firearm, own a dog while on parole, or leave the state while serving my one year parole term. One year, would be my minimum projected parole term. The two years is cut in half, pending no trouble and a good prognosis during the one year of parole. I sat in the same seat that, just two weeks prior, I had sat on when entering this institution. Though I had requested from Springfield, time and time again, a transfer from Shawnee to Sheridan's treatment program, my release was on their terms. Now that I had finally made it at Sheridan, I am told it is time to go. How ironic! It just goes to show how backwards the justice system is. There truly is no such thing as reform in the Illinois Penal system.

There isn't enough help to provide those who need treatment. I had heard that only fifteen-percent of inmates ever receive any form of rehabilitation, that offenders within Illinois are incarcerated at a rate forty times higher than any civilized country, and that Illinois faces nearly a sixty-percent recidivism rate. According to the Pew Center on The States, every ten-dollars that go into corrections in this country, nine-dollars go to prisons and only one-dollar will see its way to probation/ parole. In fact, in Illinois, for every one-dollar spent, there's five-cents spent on probation/parole.

Hell, I can see why one in thirty-one adults in the United States are under the control of the correctional systems. Without knowing these statistics, I could already feel the harshness the world held for me. I feared the day of my release. I had nothing to get me started. Not a job or any education anyone would give a damn about. Nobody can understand the bond we share behind these walls. Nobody will ever understand. I hope you will never have to. Even as I left some of the guards were taking their final cracks at us.

"Those of you who burned your bridges and are taking the bus somewhere, wait here. The bus will be arriving in about thirty minutes. For those of you who are getting picked up; that being Harnish… follow me," the officer said, directing me towards the door to the outside leading to a sidewalk which goes to the same double gates which let our bus in after a thorough inspection. Now, there are no searches, no vulgar remarks made by the officers; just a smaller entrance in the gate that the control center is nestled between. There was no more ID worn on my jacket reading "Inmate #R62100." Before being released, we were given the money left over on our books. We were not given a handshake and farewell.

I was free to go after serving two years in the Department of Corrections. One year inside a medium-maximum security prison in the southernmost tip of Illinois, probably due to overcrowding of Illinois penitentiaries. Three months of that time, I didn't have to serve but the extension was the result of a "mistake" on the part of Illinois' "wonderful" state and government employees.

As I walked outside on the other side of the fence, now looking in on a world most will never get to see or know, I am happy to feel the cool crisp air and the wind biting my face. I feel the sun as I hadn't for the past two years of my life. At that moment, I know who I am and I remember where I came from. I am not an ex-convict #R62100, drunk, drug dealer, drug user, or one of many labels given to me over the year. I am a father, son, brother, and a family member. I am, at this moment, a free man. No matter what mistakes were made, bottom line, I am just happy to be leaving.

Chapter 29

Arriving At Shawnee Correctional Center

o o o o o o o o o o o o o o o o o o o o o o o o o o o o o o

"Your secret is your prisoner; once you reveal it, you become its slave."

Solomon Ibn Gabirol

I endured a grueling eight hour bus ride in silence. There were strict rules on the bus dealing with talking. We were each shackled from our wrists and then chained to the top of the next man's seat. It was a huge chained-in conga line. There were no luxuries that might be found on a typical tour bus. The seats were not padded. They were hard plastic and you had to twist your body to fit as comfortably as possible so your knees didn't hit the seat in front of you. There were no windows to look out of except the narrow windows screened in at the top of the bus that allowed you to see the tops of the trees you passed.

About six hours later, we switched buses and a bucket was carried onto the bus in which each inmate had his turn to piss. Anyone caught talking had a good possibility of spending his next month in segregation upon arrival.

From our layover at Logan Penitentiary, about halfway to Shawnee and nestled in the small town of Lincoln, Illinois, we met up with those from southern Illinois heading north. We were then placed on another identical bus to finish the two- to three-hour ride further south to Shawnee Penitentiary. Our only stop on this portion of the trek was for lunch at Pickneyville Correctional Center; Pickneyville is widely considered a maximum security penitentiary in southern Illinois.

Upon arriving at Shawnee, the receiving units included two sides and formed concrete steps with railings that led to the upper deck of

receiving. Cells lined the two sides of the wall with a small slit in the middle where there was a screen that allowed one to see the outline of the inmate standing just behind the screen. There we could hear the whispers and calls of the other inmates. On the end closest to the control center there was a recessed brick wall on the near side with the toilets and showers where inmates were allowed to shower once a week under the observation of the guards. We sat just below the stairs on the formed concrete bench next to the phones each one of us would try to use to see if the pin numbers we received from Stateville were working. For those of us who were first time inmates, it would be another month before we would be able to contact anyone from the outside world.

We came into each penitentiary the same way. We would be checked over and our names were read off one by one each time we approached the gate of a new penitentiary, then the outside of the bus would be thoroughly inspected while another officer walked a dog around the bus. Finally, the gate would open and we would pull around to another fence which would be opened. Then we would be walked inside the penitentiary and lined up along the inside of the fence where we would be counted once again before being taken inside the receiving unit by being buzzed through sets of doors and gates before being told once again where to go.

Prior to getting our bedding, we were stripped down, lined up, and went through the motions of bending over, spreading our ass cheeks, and being humiliated by the guards before being thrown our bright yellow jump suits and bedding. At last, we would be taken to our cells in receiving where we would stay for the next two weeks while going through evaluations with internal affairs, psychologists, property, and lastly, our orientation into the facility. I sat in my cell, like every inmate, wanting to be out and among the general population where I would get a little more movement and participate in the schooling that one could take advantage of. Plus, we couldn't wait to get our hands on a cigarette.

I wasn't sure who I would know, or what to expect. As we were directed to our orientation class, I found a familiar face. I sat next to one of the guys I called John-John who was a Deuce from Elgin. He passed over a cigarette and a match for me to take back to my cell. The next morning I was given orders to get my clothing and report to Four House. I was given several pairs of light blue shirts, navy blue pants, and a change of underwear. I walked into my new home inside Four House, D-wing, cell number twenty-five. I immediately didn't like this new environment.

I walked in through the front door of the large brick building shaped like an "X". There were four wings and a central control center in the middle of each house where three officers made their daily living seated shoulder height off the ground, inside a bulletproof glass bubble.

After I was buzzed through the set of double glass doors, I approached the "bubble" to be yelled at, "Well, what the hell do you want?" I looked at them with pure hate boiling through my eyes and through pursed lips said, "Harnish." Both guards, knowing I was new, looked at me as if I were stupid and said, "Congratulations, you retard, but here we go by numbers." I glanced down at my ID and, questioning their ability to read since it was displayed on the front of my shirt said, "R62100."

They pointed to the door and called for an inmate doing laundry to help me carry my large property box and correspondence box, along with my bedding, to the corner cell where I would be living. As I entered the cell, I saw my celli. He introduced himself as Turk and said that he was a Gangster Disciple from the "Low Ends," Chicago's south side. He felt it necessary to disclose his entire life to me in a first introduction, saying that he previously served time at Pontiac where he was incarcerated for murder. He was currently on yard and commissary restriction, or "C-Grade" for a fight he had gotten into across the street at Vienna Correctional Center, a minimum-security institution. Right away, I didn't care for him. He talked too much. He acted like he had too much to prove. I could care less where he'd been or who he was.

All I knew was that I had immediately cliqued with some Latinos on the deck which made our situation even worse since he was a black GD from Chicago. He was my height, 6'1", but had a skinny build with stretch marks indicating he may have once worked out but had decreased in size, probably from the crack he'd been smoking when out in the world. He had this twitch to him, like he had Tourette's. Or maybe he had been hit in the head which, by the way he talked, may have been well-deserved. He acted like he knew everything, but based on what really came through, I would rate his IQ as barely making it as a primate.

I slid my box under the bed. Like Stateville, the metal slats were welded and bolted to the wall. Our desk was covered in newspaper taped down with the adhesive strips from deodorant and shampoo labels. There were tobacco crumbs all over the room. There were no electronics except for a half-busted radio Turk listened to. There were a couple of shelves at eye level next to the desk where each inmate could put his toiletries, Bible, or photos. In the corner by the door was the stainless steel toilet/ sink combo. Turk would do his laundry there by sticking clothes in the toilet and repeatedly flushing it. Above the sink was another metal shelf where an inmate could put his hot-pot to heat up water he used for commissary items. Fact is, this guy was all talk. He was broke. There was nobody sending him money, and the way he took care of himself and the cell, I would guess he was homeless. Still, he told a different story. He was always trying to talk about how much money he made out there and what he's got. However, nobody knew this guy, and I didn't care about anything he ever had to say.

That first day inside the cell in general population is the worst. Everyone knows you're the new guy. Everyone wants something from you. You come into this cell wanting out, but you know that as soon as this door "pops," or opens, for chow, everyone will come out looking at you asking you who you are and sizing you up. A few will stand at their window chucks, which is nothing more than a grimy screen covering a narrow opening in the door, and yell out questions for you. But, each question is double-edged. If you answer, not knowing who is talking, you could be led into a trap. If you don't answer, it could appear as though you're afraid.

Luckily, or unluckily, it wouldn't be long before we were all going to be stuck in our cells for a lock-down and then I would be moved to a new house.

It happened when I was out of my cell for our one hour free time. I was playing cards on a stainless steel table. I heard over the loud speakers, "Everyone lock it up!" It was half an hour into our free time. I heard the bottom gallery doors pop open for us to enter our cells. The upper gallery would miss their free time since the two floors alternate times twice a day. In fact, the only time you get to see the whole gallery is for the half hour you get when each wing is marched out individually for chow. The only time you get to see other inmates in different houses is when you run across them "on the walk," or sidewalks. Occasionally you are sent a "call pass" to go see the doctor or for your school's TABE test to place you in school to determine class eligibility. While leaving the housing units on that call pass, you might occasionally see another inmate out on the walk on his call pass. Another way you run into others is at church. There you will find inmates from all over the penitentiary. In fact, barely anyone goes to church to pray; they go to see others they might know and pass things to another housing unit. Otherwise, you could know someone inside Shawnee and never even know they were there. Movement is severely restricted. You can, however, see inmates from different wings in your housing unit as long as they are on the same deck, or upper/lower level as you. They will go to the same yard time or gym time as you.

I hadn't really gotten to know anyone yet, but I stood up from the card table and entered my cell for what would be a one month lock down. No inmate in the institution would be allowed to leave his cell without a call pass, and even then the inmate must be shackled and escorted. It would be another month before I would be able to call my Mom. I hadn't even gotten commissary, or been able to arrange for a television or electronics through my family. It would be three months by the time I got to hear my son's voice on the phone.

I found out the reason for the lockdown two weeks later when the "orange crush" team came barging into each cell looking for the large metal pieces gone missing out of the industry building. They would come in with their shields up and Billie-clubs drawn, yelling at those of us inside our cells to get our faces on the wall one-by-one and we would be strip searched and cuffed.

Cell by cell, we would be seated at one of the four stainless steel tables on each level while they tore apart our cells. Then we were shoved back into the cells if they were clean or taken to segregation if contraband was found. After going though so much in just a short period of time, you start to wonder.

Will you get through this? Will you ever be the same by the time you get out? I questioned whether my hands could ever be washed clean after the things I have done and the people I have hurt.

Chapter 30

A Recount Of Hardin County Work Camp

o o o o o o o o o o o o o o o o o o o o o o o o o o o o o o o o o o o

"Men are not prisoners of fate, but only prisoners of their own minds."

Franklin D. Roosevelt

In Sheridan, I had a lot of time to think about what I had been through. It was only six or seven months ago when I left Shawnee penitentiary and was sent to Hardin County Work Camp. There, I worked a hot summer picking up garbage beside a road, clearing out lots of trees, and mowing city property in nearby small towns. I was taken off road crew when it was discovered that I had a warrant out for my arrest in Carroll County, Illinois, for a possession charge the night I ended up in a hospital pumped full of narcane, a shot they give you after an overdose.When that charge was dropped due to time limitations and the non-severity of the case in accordance to the time I was already serving, I was able to return to Hardin County Work Camp and attend the penitentiaries' construction program.

There, I moved and smuggled cigarettes into the penitentiary after getting good deals on bundles of smokes. I was paying fifty dollars for nearly eighty smokes, and then turning around and selling them for a dollar or more a piece. Somehow, I even snuck through an investigation where a big package picked up off the side of the road made its way to me shy of a full package. Unfortunately, the smokes and cans of Skoal chewing tobacco were being sold too early. The situation was perceived as though my brother and his girlfriend had dropped off the contraband on their recent visit. Truth is, if it wasn't for one of the C/O's being caught red handed and getting fired for delivering a package, I could have had one of the officer's bring it in for me. That situation prompted the event we jokingly referred to as "tobacco-gate". Orange Crush came in and cleared every crevice of the penitentiary, removing and searching the air conditioning units out of each room, even digging holes in the garden and unearthing bags of tobacco based on information inmates had provided. We lost a lot of people during those times, and since Hardin County is a part of Shawnee Penitentiary, when inmates are kicked out, they are actually banked back to Shawnee Penitentiary.

Hardin County Work Camp is thirty minutes southwest of Shawnee. It is extreme minimum. You can run along a track and leave the dorm rooms that sleep ten or twelve people per room anytime you choose. There are no fences and no guard towers. There is only a mandatory count six times a day to make sure that everyone is still present.

As it turned out, I was suppose to have been placed at Hardin the moment I entered Shawnee, but because of another screw-up, I was kept at Shawnee. After all the letters Mom and I wrote to Springfield explaining that I was improperly placed and requesting a move, it was not Springfield at all that resulted in my transfer. It was a teacher in my heating ventilation and air conditioning class who questioned such a harsh placement from DUIs that got me transferred. In Hardin County, after dodging the situation with selling cigarettes, I received seven tickets in two months for minor violations like smoking, breaking room restriction, and being out of uniform. The work camp reminded me more of military school than anything else.

Still, like any prison, you find your clique. I fell in with the Latin Folks at first, but I didn't know anybody there. In fact, the whole act of everybody trying to be someone they weren't got old. I had one good friend at Hardin. Rolo was a well-toned black guy, littered in tattoos, that was from Chicago. He was different. This was a man who lived as he spoke. He was driven in life. His case was different than most in Hardin County Work Camp. He was there for manslaughter, but I never thought of him in that way. He was in the military, has a daughter whom he dearly wants to go home to, and he doesn't give up on life. We would often walk the track day after day after finishing weight lifting and just talk about philosophy, religion, and life. We would ponder business ventures and escape to a different place in the corners of our minds. He made the work camp a better place for me. Jokingly, I would call him my consigliore during my troubles with selling cigarettes and dodging bullets with the guards. He was the voice of reason I needed to hear during those times.

I constantly moved my stash spots and used other boxes for a "safe house" when the guards would come in and search my property. Everything had to match up to my commissary receipts. Otherwise, I would have another ticket for trafficking and trading. I also kept aside a different box I called my "re-up box". I used it for purchasing the next bundle of cigarettes. I had almost gotten myself into a situation when a Latin Dragon from Chicago rightfully defended himself and smacked some young black kid after being spit on. Unfortunately, my name was brought up in the mix for no reason.

I liked the freedom of Hardin County, but at the same time, it can go straight to the head with the mix there. Everyone is always telling on someone, and sooner or later, you have the guards moving in on you. Once it gets to that point, it is only a matter of time before they have you banked back to Shawnee.

In Hardin, I got called into my counselor's office to speak to my Grandma one last time before she died from ALS. My brother also left to go to South Korea where he teaches English. I hated missing out on seeing these two people. During my time inside, I rekindled relationships I had lost with many people during the years since my seventh grade.

Now the moment has arrived. I decided it was a perfect day to be released. I stood in the parking lot and thought about my younger brother in South Korea. I wished he was here so that I could tell him how much he meant to my mental strength in making it through. I also thought of my Grandma. I wanted so much for her to know that I made it out and would continue down a path of righteousness. She would often write to me regarding the Scriptures in the Bible, hoping that I would find comfort in the spiritual presence it provides. She once thought that I would be a minister when I grew older. She thought I had a special place in life after I was in a coma from being hit by a pick-up truck when I was six years old. I was one of God's miracles. I guess I owe it to her to prove that I will live life on life's terms and according to the Golden Rule. She always meant so much to me. I miss my Grandma, and it hurts to know that I will not see her again.

I remember one of my favorite scriptures from I Corinthians, Chapter 13, verse 11. It states, "When I was a child, I spoke as a child, I thought as a child, and reasoned as a child. But when I grew up, I put away childish things." I hope that I have come out of this experience a humble man. I would find out later, by some sort of fate or mere coincidence, the day I was released, happened to be the date of my Grandpa's birthday.

I know now that I am not the same person as I was before. I don't know who I am or where I am going. And yet, I am happy knowing I am not who I use to be. I still question, however, whether my hands can ever be washed clean after the things I have done and the people I have hurt.

Chapter 31

New Cell, New Wing, New Job

o o o o o o o o o o o o o o o o o o o o o o o o o o o o o o

"On average, drug prisoners spend more time in federal prison than rapists, who often get out on early release because of the overcrowding in prison caused by the drug war."

Michael Badnarik

A month of wrestling with my mind and peering out of my two-foot wide, barred cell window had me restless. I spent the July 4th looking out into the yard area outside my window and thinking of my deceased Grandpa and how much he loved this holiday. I remembered the last July 4th that I spent at Potawatomie Park with my Mom, Allena, and Damian. Even though Damian slept through most of the fireworks, it was a perfect day; a day I still remember. Now, I live through my past. I remember all the good and bad, and I feel horrible about how things have turned out now. I am scared about what may come.

I sat up late the next night, brainstorming ideas and writing business plans for when I get out. I started out with small goals like taking Damian fishing, to larger goals I hoped to attain like owning a business. I searched everything: other inmates' actions and my own thinking, as if there were a psychological key I had to find that would explain all my imperfections. I relived my life a day at a time, experiencing every moment again and again, mentally analyzing everything as if I were my own psychologist. I questioned my motives on wanting success and tried to figure out my drive for it. Was it for me? Was I looking for someone else's approval? I worked through every move I made. Even though some of my actions were questionable, I justified them as a sociological reaction to my current harsh environment.

My situation escalated toward the end of the lockdown when Turk tried to demand that I purchase certain items out of commissary that would suit him. In a way, he may have been correct, but it was the fact that I didn't want him to feel like he had reins over me. When I denied him that right, he looked at me and slammed his fist on the top bunk in a fit of rage. I immediately shot up off of my bottom bunk and jumped to my feet.

"Do what you do then, nigga!" I yelled at him as I stood tall next to the door and toilet.

The cell was small, so it only allowed for a mere three feet of movement. With both of us standing, we were infringing on one another's personal space, making the whole thing uncomfortable. I was tired of him. Whatever his decision was, I was ready to go, just to get the fight out of the way. I was tired of being perceived as just another soft white boy. I stood there glaring at him, fully prepared. He turned and lowered his voice, implying that my purchases on items should include tobacco. Our purchases were limited since we were on lock-down. Since it was my first purchase, I was loading up on toiletries.

The following day, I heard the door pop and the guards walked into our cell. I looked at Turk, thinking he told the guards about our argument. I was mad that he had ratted.

"R62100?" the guard asked, looking at the ID's displayed at the end of our bed.

"Yeah," I replied, more as a question about what this could be about than a statement that I was that inmate.

"R62100, pack your shit up."

"Where am I going?" I asked while getting my shit together.

"Just get your shit together and follow me," he snapped back sternly. As it turned out, I was not heading to seg, but to One House. At One House, inmates are assigned to work or school. There I moved into a cell on 1-C-59. I walked in and felt relieved when I saw my celli. He was a deep-spoken white guy with a southern drawl. He turned out to be from Texas. Like me, he was here on a DUI conviction and had been fighting the state for a transfer. Not only that, but he had a television and all the electronics. Plus, John-John, known to some as Puppet, and another Deuce from Elgin, Kool-Aid, was on the deck. I liked this deck. My celli went by Tex. He was a man with a big ego, but I found it easy to talk to him. He gave me the names of the people I should write to about transferring. He kept the cell clean and knew how to cook.

Shortly after I moved into the cell I placed an order for my first commissary. I was also placed on a job assignment in the officers'

commissary where I worked inside a cage serving and ringing up the officer's food. I retrieved their food in my caged-in convenience store and exchanged money and food through a serving hole. I worked from six o' clock at night to eight or nine the following morning for five days out of the week. Even though there were lock-downs due to fights that arose throughout the penitentiary and a rape that occurred in Two House, I was always able to go to work since the officers always needed their food. It was also nice because it made my time go by fast, but it was a pain in other ways.

I never got any sleep since the gallery would be flooded with noise during the day from inmates yelling out of their cells, count checks, and dayroom noise when the decks were out for their free time. I missed out on yard and gym since I was sleeping during the day. I missed calling my Mom since our hours didn't mesh. Before I knew it, the bad started outweighing the good and I wanted out of the job. I hadn't gotten to know a soul on the gallery except for my celli and those from past prison contact. Then before I knew it, my friend John-John went back to Kane County on a court writ and Kool-Aid was moved. Unfortunately, I Couldn't just quit my job without landing myself in seg. All I could do was keep writing the state and try to get my transfer, hoping that someone would realize I was in a disciplinary joint that houses inmates for crimes such as larger drug crimes, attempted murder, and murder charges.

I found my way out of the job the morning I received my call pass for a nine o' clock appointment for my TABE test, a test to see whether you need mandatory schooling provided to every inmate to help inmates once released. I knew that if I failed the test, I would be placed in mandatory schooling and be taken off the job. In school I could work towards good time for every ninety days of class. I sat down that morning tired and exhausted after a long night; a job that paid only twenty five dollars a month. I set my ID on the front desk of the classroom and grabbed the pencil that had to be accounted for so that inmates wouldn't steal it to make shanks.

"This is a timed test. You will have thirty minutes to complete this first section. Continue on until the thirty minutes is up, or until the test booklet tells you to stop. Do not get out of your seats during the test and keep your eyes on your own test. Any questions?" the instructor asked.

Of course, for most inmates, we were not paying attention to what she said. We watched her hips slightly move from side to side as her slender body and athletic curves traveled the classroom. She was gorgeous. Her

brown hair fell over her shoulders and brushed the side of her face. It was amazing that someone like her would work in a place like this.

"How long is this going to take?" I asked. It was as if I were rubbing sand paper together with each blink of the eye.

"This will take us until lunch," she nicely answered back.

I hated doing this to her. I had a nice disposition toward the teachers since my mom was an educator. But I was beaten, tired, and just didn't care what would happen to me. I was so tired from working that segregation Sounded like a nice break from it all.

I stood up and walked to the front of the class room muttering, "I can't do this. I've got to go."

She hesitated, unsure what to say or do. She sat behind her desk and said, "Don't do this. Just sit there, you don't even have to do anything. If you leave, I will have to write a ticket."

I just looked at her sympathetically and replied, "You've got to do what you've got to do. I have to go to bed."

I was sure I would be cuffed up and taken to seg on my walk back to the housing unit. I left the classroom, walked right by the officer's desk outside in the hallway, made my way down the stairs and pushed the glass door open taking me to the winding sidewalks past the chow hall and the commissary to the left, and took a right into my housing unit and into my cell where I slept until that evening when I would go to work all over again.

The following morning when the guards made their shift change and that morning's lieutenant came in, he told me that he threw away my ticket and would have done the same thing in my shoes. It was kind of him and, what was even better, was the fact that I had voluntarily scored a zero on my TABE score so I would have to attend mandatory schooling. I made it out of the job without going to segregation after all. Plus, because I see the teachers come in every morning as I empty the garbage outside of the gates and fences while the prison marksman trains a gun on me in case I decide to run into the vast Shawnee national forest across the way, I was able to convince one of the head teachers, Pam, to squeeze me in the class quickly. In just a week, I was out of the job, inside a new housing unit, and still writing the state to get out of this penitentiary. I was moved over to Two House and placed inside a cell with a man who has served over twenty years for murder. He would have a major impact on the way I carry myself. The important thing is, I am able to move on with my life.

Chapter 32

Mom... I Am Home Now

o o o o o o o o o o o o o o o o o o o o o o o o o o o o o o

"There is no wrong reason for doing the right thing."

Unknown

"Mom..." I uttered to myself.

This would be the first time I would be able to hug her, be with her, outside the scrutiny and constant surveillance of the guards inside the penitentiaries' visiting rooms. Too many times in the past two years, I had to remain guarded and preoccupied about those around me while my Mom visited. Too many times, I had to sit across from her at a steel table and keep my hands on the table at all times, allowed only an embrace at the beginning and end of the visit. This would be the first time in two years that I would not be strip-searched before I walked into a room mounted with cameras to see my Mom.

Aside from the visits, however, my family and I had been able to form something that only prison could have brought to my life. There was no more hiding anything from them. I had even opened up to my father. For the first time since I was a child, I feel like I had built an honest foundation for my relationships to grow on. These are the things I take with me now that I am leaving the penitentiary. My family served time right there next to me the entire time. They wrote letters and sent money so that I could enjoy the little things in the penitentiary that makes the end of the day palatable. Though it is nothing much to a free man, I was able to look forward to cooking and making meals with a group of inmates. In a way, I miss some of those times. Not the aspect of being locked up, but I fear that so much of what I have built will collapse now. I am just another member of society, still labeled, with all the stresses the world has to offer. I feel like, out here, people are too wrapped up in their everyday lives to see the importance of those around them. This is what the penitentiary gave to me, the realization that no moment in life is trivial.

In a way, standing here in this parking lot at Sheridan, all I want is back inside. I feel like everything in life is as it should be. I have found my family in the truest sense of the word. I am not sure what awaits me out here in the real world anymore. In a way I am being reborn all over again. I have a clean slate and I can try to leave my mark. This time things will be different though. This time, perhaps, I will just leave my slate blank and let someone else draw me a picture. My plans have changed since my unexpected release from prison. I didn't want to go back to Kane County. I didn't want to see old friends. Not because they are bad people, but because I know the mixture of us together is an explosive combination. But, because of the unexpected release, my Mom's was the only approved parole destination. Otherwise I had planned to live with my father, far away from Kane County, knowing the dangers and fears that exist in Kane County. I was lost, confused, and unsure of my path from here.

I am unable to see past the ten yards in front of me. Except, those ten yards are all that matter right now because waiting for me at the end of those ten yards is my Mom. She is now a principal, and she still has her lessons to dish out. She sat there, waiting for me, by her car. My body was still tense from all the time inside the penitentiary. I walked like an inmate, with a cool swagger that masked the beaten and humiliated convict behind it. I walked right up to my Mom as she smiled, happy to have me back in her arms. I held back the tears when she said those words to me that I had wanted to hear for so long.

"You made it," she said softly as she squeezed me, nestling her brown hair against my chest.

I didn't know what I was going to do, where I was going to go at the end of it all, or which path I would take in life. I guess right now, the important thing is, I am able to move on with my life.

Chapter 33

Convicted Murderer, Mentor, And Friend

o o o o o o o o o o o o o o o o o o o o o o o o o o o o o o o o o

"Blessed are they who see beautiful things in humble places where other people see nothing."

Camille Pissarro

As my week's activity sheet changed from a job assignment to school as primary, I was soon following the Two House runner who brought a large dolly for me to put my property on and wheel it down the sidewalk and barren grass, passing one of the two or three trees inside the penitentiary walls. I had a new home on the upper deck and corner cell nearest the window for the officer's view on D wing of Two House.

I did not like my cellie from day one. This fat, unkempt, white guy had the look of child molester all over him. He resembled Cookie the Clown from the Bozo Show when I was a kid. I nicknamed him "Cookie" due to his odd penguin walk and look. Cookie worked in the kitchen and didn't shower, making our cell smell like rotten food and ass. He was missing several teeth, but he would try to say he was a hitman who made a million for the mob. He talked about his pet bobcat and tiger and other stupid crap that even the most gullible person wouldn't buy. Plus, to make him hated throughout the gallery, everyone knew that he would go to internal affairs and "trick" on others. That was made obvious when I marked his ID and he came back from IA saying he had actually gone to B of I, or Bureau of Identification, to get a new ID. The mark I made was still there and the old date of the ID was displayed on the back side. It was even more ironic that the young black kid who slapped him behind closed doors was taken to seg the following day.

It took awhile to get out of that cell. I was drawing when I heard the cell door's electric lock pop back. I knew Cookie would be coming up the stairs to return to his bed after working that morning in the kitchen. What he didn't expect, was that all his belongings would be outside the cell door. I pushed all his toiletries and a towel on the floor and told him to get his ass in the shower or we would have problems when he came into the cell. The guards give you time to shower after any job assignment. When he kept coming in to the cell smelling like onions, I decided I had enough of his rotting teeth and crusty clothes that hadn't seen laundry detergent for years. Selling onions and kitchen vegetables was his hustle, along with making cards for others off of tracing patterns he had accumulated over the years. He had to work hard for the little he would get in his box, so I saw that as my way to get him out of the cell. We worked out an arrangement that he would pay me eighty dollars in food items for a set of paint brushes I would purchase for him after debts were paid for some sixty dollars. Once purchased, I set up the cell to be robbed when I left the door unlatched. His tracing patterns, food, and paintbrushes were stolen. Oddly the paint brushes worked their way back in my possession along with some of the food. I think he knew it was a set up, but I didn't care. He couldn't prove it, and when the guard came to report it, I was the one in possession of the receipt for the paintbrushes. Since trafficking and trading is illegal, there was nothing he could do. I had stripped from him his main hustle.

It took physical threats to have me moved some eight cells down. As I carried my property and set them up in this new cell, I immediately noticed the 6'6", 250 lb muscled black man with a shaved head and long goatee. This man had served over twenty years for strong armed robbery and murder. He was transferred here after bouncing around penitentiaries all over Illinois. He served a majority of his time behind the wall at Stateville maximum security penitentiary. There he held a position for the Gangster Disciples back when the joints were inmate run. During those times, guards would ask the inmates for permission to come on the gallery. He was intimidating, but more than that, he was intriguing. Past his size and charges, this was now a man who had completely changed. He proved to be a good friend and brother. Every inmate finds his way to make it through the time. The saying goes, "Do your time, don't let time do you."

This man, who now goes by his Muslim name, Haleem, found his way by devoting his life to Allah. He was sincere in his kind actions and words. He was not a man of violence or loud spoken words. Haleem was the best celli I ever had. I learned more from him during my time in that cell than I did in any class or from any person elsewhere in the penitentiary. He shared with me the words of Allah and the importance of family and faith. He seeks forgiveness for the terrible actions that caused his incarceration at age eighteen. He now states that he must save someone's life to even attempt to be forgiven for his actions. The cell was immaculate and, though his family is now gone and help is void for him, he didn't beg or want anything except for his five prayers a day. I was grateful to share my things with this man. What I could do for him would pale in comparison to the things he showed me.

Another thing every inmate learns quickly is that life ceases to exist inside these walls, but outside, life continues. Relationships rarely endure this trial. Only existing over letters and almost void of any human emotion, intimacy crumbles into the arms of another man for the wife or girlfriend outside. For me it was my ex-wife Allena. I had rarely kept in contact with her. For the first time in three months, I called to get the latest on my son, the son I watched grow and flourish through pictures sent to me, only to hear that the mother of my son was pregnant with the child of another man. I am not sure what I expected to ever happen between the two of us. I enjoyed the mail I would occasionally get from her. It was nice to have another person out in the world to bounce ideas off of. But she moved on. Perhaps it was the fact that there is someone else that is a part of my son's life. Yet, that day my heart was forever tucked away somewhere dark. I had given up on the "you and me" of things. Now there is only "us and them". I held on to the words and advice from my friend, Haleem, and continued to move on, spending time with the only world I knew. I made a life for myself behind these bars, just as others have outside these walls.

Time can move fast in a penitentiary if you just forget about the day you're in and live in the moment. The second that you get too wrapped up in the here and now and forget about who you are outside is the moment that captures you and you catch yourself in stupid scenarios with the possibility of six more months added to your sentence. Prison is as easy as you choose to make it, or as hard as you want it to be. The challenge is the letting go of everything you once knew. The freedom you once experienced in daydreams and the silent nights lying on your bed slip away into the dark nights. Dreams are no longer dreamed and the only hope you have is not to wind up in the politicking that takes place in every corner and every cell in the penitentiary.

Telephone calls become more and more sparse, and letters become shorter as your thoughts and plans for the future are as caged in as you are at the moment. My hopes of retrieving the life I left behind diminished just as the succulent taste of buttered lobster turns to a bitter kiss by the night's end. The clock on the far wall that can barely be seen outside the small screen on our cell doors only tells us when the next mystery meal is served. Other than that, mail, for those lucky few, is the only thing that is worth looking forward to.

Time is for people with plans, a schedule to adhere to. Calendars are never seen inside a cell, since tomorrow is marked only in the imagination of one's mind. Perhaps, only a television program may mark a highlight in the day of an inmate. Many will "bug up," or go nuts, if they can't deal with the nothingness that surrounds the underlying attitude of this place. The constant insults from the guards and the traps they purposely try to set up for you only proved that their lives are as routine and boring as ours. In jail, I could count a month as gone by through the court dates. Here, I knew when I had a reply from a letter, and it would be a month before they had my response. It would take the mail fifteen days to reach the cell door from the date it was sent out.

So, each month, I would sit and write my letters to my family. Once a month, a letter would go out to Springfield so that I could get to a minimum security institution where they had classes in drug counseling, EMT training, and other programs that better suited my interests than the heating ventilation and air conditioning (HVAC) class I had enrolled in.

It would take me at least five months to complete a contract due to the constant lock downs issued for fights and union problems with the guards and administrators. There were always rifts between the two about pay and time off, along with the most popular concern, understaffing of the facility. Honestly, inmates don't step out of line too often because nobody wants to spend more time in this hell. Plus, if you don't win your fight, it could take the guards and nurses twenty minutes to reach the cell or gallery. Imagine what can be done in twenty minutes. Sure there were problems from time to time, but then again, close yourself off from outside contact and live with a group of guards who insult you and you may lash out from time to time throughout the years.

Most inmates are serving at least four years; many are looking to upwards of eight or twelve years. With that much time, you can learn patience and figure out how to do things over a course of time. You can befriend a guard so that he may turn a blind eye to things, learn how to give tattoos, or learn a new language. One used to be able to obtain degrees inside, but due to improper funding and the rest of the country generally not giving a shit, programs have pretty much been tossed. There is a fine distinction made between the "us" and "you" in the penitentiary. After two years, I no longer feel that I am one of you. Truth is, I no longer know where I belong. Perhaps I am not meant to be one of "you," but back where there is only "us."

Chapter 34

Damian, My son, Daddy Is Here Now

o o o o o o o o o o o o o o o o o o o o o o o o o o o o o o

"Recounting of a life story, a mind thinking aloud leads one inevitably to the consideration of problems which are no longer psychological but spiritual."

Dr. Paul Tournier

I rode home with Mom, down the streets I had once traveled a long time ago. As we came closer to what would be my new home, I barely recognized the area. New buildings had been built and the once quiet countryside was disappearing. Everything had changed; I had changed. I sat in the passenger seat, looking out the window at the world I am oddly familiar with. I took in all the smells, sights, and wonders it had to offer. I looked at the odd devices I was not familiar with, like the iPod resting between my Mom and me. I looked at the cell phone that looked nothing like the ones I had seen before.

"Do you want to call your brothers?" Mom asked excitedly, wanting the world to know that I am free and again one of "you."

"Okay," I replied as I picked up the cell phone.

It had been a long time. I tried to figure out how to call my brother, but the phone was so new to me, I didn't quite know how to work it.

Mom saw me struggling and softly said, "Here, honey, let me do that for you."

It was frustrating and humbling. As I left a message for Jason, my throat tightened. I couldn't believe I was really calling my brother from a cell phone inside a car that doesn't have bars, but instead a window where I can view the world. I felt free. I just wanted to have my Mom pull over so that I could walk nowhere, anywhere, just walk through the fields and soak it in. When

Jason called back, I could only give short answers. I couldn't say too much and let him hear my voice tremble. I have waited a long time to experience this moment.

"How are you doing?" Mom asked, as my mind wandered off for some time.

"I'm okay Mom… I'm alright," I said, unsure what these feelings were.

"How about we stop at the grocery store before we head home?" she asked as we came closer to home.

"Okay Mom, let's go," I said with long pauses, softly spoken with slight nods of the head.

It was all so different. Inside the grocery store, I pushed the cart around still wearing the clothes I was released in, thinking everyone knew where I had just come from. I clenched the cart in front of me as if it were a barrier between me and everyone else.

Mom rested her hand on my shoulder and asked me, "What would you like?"

I just shrugged my shoulders and said, "Whatever you want Mom… I don't know." I couldn't believe how easy it was for everyone to just pick whatever they wanted off of a shelf and put it into the cart. "These people don't realize how lucky they are to do this simple thing, grocery shopping," I thought.

When we got home, I put the groceries on the kitchen table and helped put everything away. Mom looked at me and asked if I had called Allena.

"I'm not ready yet," I replied. "I just want to take things slow and get adjusted," I added, as I stood still next to the kitchen table and looked around the house.

Everything was how I remembered. It was still the same house. Memories flooded my mind about the things I had done, the good times I had in this house. I remembered other things too: the day the gun was pulled out in the house my freshman year of high school; the day a friend broke his leg after a fight in the front yard. Then I remembered… I remembered this was almost exactly the same spot I stood when I turned my back on my boy and walked out the door. My God, how would I ever be forgiven for that night? I haven't held Damian in two years. I don't think he could even recognize me now. How can I face him? Guilt came over me as if it were just yesterday. Everything I had taken for granted meant so much more to me now. My family, my career, my driver's license. What is to become of me? What am I to do? Mom saw the weary look on my face, and she came over to me and gave me a hug.

She squeezed me and said, "Welcome home Ryan. It will be all right." Tears started building up in my eyes and the world melted behind the tears.

Then drip… drip… drip. The tears escaped from my eyes. I turned from Mom, wiping the tears away. I stood there naked, transparent, my guard was down and, for the first time in over two years, I cried. Everything inside of me was coming out. I didn't know if I was happy or sad about my release.

Nothing made my place in this world more evident than two days later when I called Allena.

"Allena, what's going on?" I said, as though it were like any other day.

"I am coming out to see you soon," she remarked, unaware that I had just called from the house.

"Why not today?" I asked.

"They told me you had to be there for a month before you could get visits."

"That's true, Allena, if I were still at Sheridan," I remarked, still in a calm and smooth tone.

"What! Where are you?" She exclaimed.

"I am at Mom's house. They made a mistake, and I'm released now," I said with a hint of excitement.

"We're coming out now!" she happily exclaimed and hung up the phone.

About an hour later the door bell rang and in came Allena, with her current boyfriend, her eight-month-old baby girl, Layla, whose father is out of the picture, and my pride and joy who was almost three years old.

I sat at the kitchen table and looked at my son, taking in how beautiful he is. His blue eyes looked around the house, searching for Grandma. He buried his face in his mother's thigh, leaving his thick brown hair facing me.

"He looks just like me," I thought to myself. "God, I love that boy," once again, to myself.

I wanted to hug him, but I was afraid of his reaction. I was worried that he may cry or be afraid of me. I just sat there and stared at him, embracing the moment.

"Damian, that's your Daddy," Allena said to him, as he turned his head showing me his little cheeks and big blue eyes.

"Why don't you take Daddy to the pond and show him how you feed the ducks," she said to our son. He brightened up and said, "Okay. Come on, Daddy, let's go."

At that moment, I knew I hadn't lost my boy. Our time was just beginning. We went out across the street to the pond where the ducks swim. We tossed out the pieces of bread and I watched the moment unfold in front of my eyes. I stood behind Damian and knelt down, wrapping my arms around him. I looked out over the pond, and then turned my gaze to him and whispered, "I love you, Damian."

Before returning to the house, I jumped on the neighbor's trampoline with him, and then he showed me how he liked to be pushed on the swing. Once home, it was only moments before I heard the "Ding!" It was the door bell. I wasn't expecting anyone. I opened up the door to see a small woman standing on the other side. She looked as though she could pack as much in her attitude as in her punch. She had a gun at her side and displayed that copper badge on her jacket which might as well read, "I am not your friend."

"Hi, I'm Deb, the parole officer assigned to your case. May I come in?" she didn't so much ask, but insisted.

As we sat at the kitchen table, she surveyed the situation and saw all the others and asked, "Who are they?"

I pointed them out saying, "That is my son, Damian, his mother, my ex, Allena, her boyfriend, and her daughter, Layla."

She looked at me for a minute. I shrugged my shoulders as if there were an understanding to what she was thinking.

"Is the other one yours?" she asked.

"No," I replied confidently." She was born when I was locked up."

"Is that her father?" She added.

"No," I said again softly.

"That doesn't bother you?" She asked, worried about any domestic problems that may arise at some point.

"No, I don't mind," I said easily.

As we looked over my paperwork, indicating no parole plans except to remain in contact with her, she saw that a mistake had been made.

I looked at her and then added, "Yeah, they messed up my calculation sheet and I was held for over three extra months that I didn't have to serve."

She looked at me and added, "It is rare, but I have heard of that happening before." I glared at her, heated from assuming she was like all the guards I have known for the past two years, and said, "I will be talking to a lawyer about this one," referring to the mistake on the part of the state of Illinois.

She just looked at me and smirked, saying, "Get in line."

As we went through the rest of the paperwork and talked over the grants available for ex-cons to acquire an education, I shot down everything she had to say.

I snapped back, "I don't want any more education. I graduated college and look what it did for me. I can't work in my profession anymore. College is a waste."

She looked at me with the same stoic pose she had maintained since she came in and said, "What are you going to do for work?"

Before I could answer she continued, "Here are places that hire felons that..."

I cut her off again, saying, "What? Bagging groceries, fast food, or working in a factory? I'm not doing it."

She stood up to see herself out. I had picked up Damian and held him in my arms while walking her out to her car.

She stood by her car and remarked, "You know, you did this to yourself?"

I looked at her, committing a homicide inside my head, and replied, "And for that, you have taken my life away. Tell me, what stops me from simply going back and doing my parole time inside?" Her eyes widened, thinking to herself that I will simply be another one; one of the nearly sixty-percent that hold up the recidivism rate by returning to the joint shortly after release.

She turned her head as she entered the car and replied, "Your reason's looking right at you," pointing to my son who was sitting in my arms just looking at me and stroking my face.

I entered the house, no more sure about myself than when I went into the penitentiary. I didn't know what to do. I had to get down to the DMV and work on getting my license back. Maybe that will provide me with some answers. Truth is, I no longer know where I belong. Perhaps I am not meant to be one of "you," but back where there is only "us."

Chapter 35

Help From Unexpected People At Unexpected Times

o o o o o o o o o o o o o o o o o o o o o o o o o o o o o o o o o o

"Do the best you can, where you are, with what you have, in the time you have."

African American Proverb

I was working towards my HVAC certificate and trying to get some more good time so that my sentence would further be reduced when my instructor, Mack, came over to me and asked to talk to me in his office.

"Yeah," I said, walking into his office, unsure what this was about. I assumed it was about some missing glass slides that had been lifted out of one of the drawers that held a microscope. I guess someone thought the glass slides would make for some use somewhere. Whether I knew who took them or not, my answer would be the same in either case. He sat in his chair along side the large garage we used as a work area and classroom.

"Ryan," he said, surprising me by using my first name, "what are you in here for?"

After telling him and explaining that I have no idea why I was here at Shawnee a year after requesting, time and time again, that I be transferred, he said, "I was talking to Pam and, if you want to go, we could get you over to Hardin County Work Camp." He continued, "It is a much nicer place than here, and they offer good time if you get into the construction tech class they offer."

I looked at him in disbelief. I can't believe that after all the letters I have written, and after I had seen the counselor on numerous occasions, it is a teacher who comes to my aid. Each one of these teachers seemed to genuinely care about each inmate who showed a willingness to improve. I agreed to go and, shortly after, Pam stopped me and said, "Don't worry. I'll get you pre-enrolled into the construction tech class so it shouldn't take that long to get you in."

I guess some days you receive a blessing in the oddest of places. It might be people you meet, places you go, or simply something said or done. In my last weekend at Shawnee, while I was glad to be leaving the institution, I will always remember some of the people I met there. Haleem was a great man, in spite of what he had done in a previous life. Then there was "old man Hill" who had fought tooth and nail to have a surgery done, but the state was unwilling to pay for it, resulting in complications that severely decreased his expected life span. He was released four months after fighting with the "powers that be", but in the end, it was four months too late. He, too, was a good man in a bad place.

Too many of the courts and laws have pushed people who are good people into a situation where help cannot be found. Not to say that all crimes should go unpunished. In fact, I will never complain that I was locked up for my errors, but there should be help, alternatives, and/or rehabilitation. I will miss those people whom I met; those people that have left a mark on my life.

I was convinced I would leave Shawnee only when I was heading home, but leaving here earlier gave me hope that some things are possible. That there are good people who step up to help in the oddest places; people that see individuals for who they are.

After I left Shawnee, my Mom wrote a letter to both Pam and Mack, thanking them for their help. I left the penitentiary in the small white van for the thirty minute ride to Hardin County Work Camp. The feeling generated in that short ride made me feel like a free man. I sat looking out the window at the flowers budding and lush green trees sprawling overhead, and I thought to myself, "This is going to be a great birthday." In the midst of everything, things can get better.

Chapter 36

Realization That I Am A Work In Progress

o o o o o o o o o o o o o o o o o o o o o o o o o o o o o o o o o o

"My Lord! Grant me from thee good offspring; surely thou art the hearer of prayer. (The family of Imran 3.38)"

Quran

I have had my fair share of disappointments since I've been out. Upon visiting the DMV, I was told that for the remainder of my life, I will never be able to have any driving privileges again. I realize that the life I hoped to once live may never be reached; that I may never work as a funeral director or embalmer again. I realize that I may never get another shot at owning my own funeral home. I may never be the husband and father in a not-so-typical happy family.

Every night when I go to bed I ponder what my next move will be. For a week after I came home, I sat on the couch and questioned whether I should see what some of the guys were up to. My life could have gone many ways at that point. I bounced around ideas on leaving the country or, perhaps, joining the military in hopes of a new life that will help me to support my son. But, the thought of leaving him eats away at me. More than anything though, I spent that first week praying for forgiveness for the things I have done. I imagine my Grandma and Grandpa looking down on me with the other family members that have passed away.

I now have a great relationship with my son, my father, and the rest of my family. I may never be rich in gold and silver, but not all riches in life can be weighed. I take things a day at a time and live life on life's terms. I may never be able to change the world or be someone great, but I speak at high schools and other youth venues in the hope that I may reach just one person and change his or her life. Each convict, if honest, would do things differently given the opportunity to change the past.

However, life outside is difficult. There are no consistencies in my life these days. I am a father, but I often fear that the day may come when I will have to leave in order to support my son. Jobs are far away and few for guys like me. I have been shot down for employment in several places. The speeches I give at high schools will one day wear thin, and my story will become old. I have sought work in the funeral profession only to learn that I am unemployable because of my inability to drive for the remainder of my life. Even the thought of going back to college and switching my degree to something else seems to not be an easy route since I must receive waivers from the Professional Board of Regulations.

I have considered nursing, but seeking approval from federal agencies since I would be around medications would be difficult. I doubt a man with my background would ever be approved. I am unable to be a teacher or work on school grounds without a waiver from Springfield, Illinois. I thought of working on the oil rigs doing offshore drilling, only to find that these jobs are very hard to find. I have tried opening a business within my hometown to find that securing a loan is nearly impossible without collateral or tax returns for the last few years.

Money has all but disappeared. I've had to seek out public aid in order to make it through this past year, and in less than a month, I will put in for release from parole. It's been hard to spread a message of hope for people like me from day to day since, at times, I feel excommunicated from this country.

Dad will say to me often, "Why not move into the city? Somewhere where a car doesn't matter? You can take the train or other public transportation." I feel that if I were to do that, the cost of living is high inside the city and even finding a factory or retail job would not cover the expenses. I will have child support, rent, transportation costs, and living expenses. In the end, I will have no time with my son, and I will struggle day to day. Why should I stay here and never get anywhere? I could go to any country and do that. At least then, I would have the satisfaction of traveling to a new place with new options.

I often think to myself, "Why not just join the military? Or just escape and go work in another country? At least then, perhaps, I can drive and renew my funeral director/ embalmer license. Damian will understand as he becomes older. He will see the importance of money as he looks toward college, a car, or needs something I cannot give him right now."

Fact is, I sometimes feel like I finally understand who I am and what truly matters to me, only to realize that it may be too late. I still need some work and polishing around the edges but that is me, and I am a work in progress.

I have to stop sometimes and remember all over again what I do have. I have my family back. I have been able to spend time with Jason since he came back from South Korea. I have spent time with Dav as he continues to try and help me with projects and business ideas. I am thankful to have these times with my son, Damian, and enjoy holidays outside the confines of a cell and in the arms of those I love. And I am thankful that I have come out of the penitentiary and crawled out from underneath my past, happy that some stains don't pass through the fabric of life.

Random Writings of a Convict

By: Ryan Harnish

How will I be remembered…
The quiet man unknown,
The lonely man that walks alone,
The simple man with much on mind,
The popular man who's very kind,
The sentimental man through which will not die,
Or shall I be just a man who let an opportunity pass him by?

Did you ever experience…
Earthly whispers dressed in black?
A tear over soft rose cheeks?
Tired, darkened, eyes with a starlight's glimmer?
Heaven was upon you and all around you.

This is not my life that you see,
It is but a figment of your memory.
How did it come to this?
What of life s lessons did I miss?
Continue on and leave me be.
Give me the key to my shackles that shall set me free.

Let not the sky rain upon thy-self,
And clear the clouds that hover over thee.
Brush aside the shadows that stay,
And forget thy winters, but a summer's day.

It comes in waves,
Like a musical note.
Sometimes a pause,
Leaving a great gap or emptiness.
Sometimes the pitch is high,
So high it hurts.
They come and go,
No note too weak, no record or song greater.

Who was I…
I was the sun when things were bright.
I was the warmth during the cold moon's light.
I was the rosebud allowing spring to grow,
And now I am through, lying beneath the snow.

When the moon next meets the sun,
Will my star still shine?
Shall thy own divine still pluck her strings?
Will the music still ring?
Or shall I sing a song forever still long
Called "loneliness to be"

I lurk in the shadows of open doors,
And creep upon cracks on old wood floors.
My odor, that of rotten meat,
Yet, my taste, that of something sweet.
My humor, subtle but there,
And my gift which none compares.

This is my life.
A twisted joke,
A small white lie,
A once kind heart now lies to die.
This is my life,
This is how I feel,
Cards have been dealt,
And I the raw deal.
Now, stripped of pride,
And full of hate,
You ask me how,
Yet all too late.
But where to begin,
I am what you see.
This is my life,
A product of sin.

Son: I made my peace 'n' stayed seated.
I watched you leave, but it aint right,
Heart whisperin', "Come back here please."
And when I got up,
You left me again.
Somehow leavin' me a stronger man.
"Why'd you leave me Dad
I needed you Dad,
Maybe someday I'll understand"
Father: Son, I'm sorry we don't have the relationship we should have had.
It was a decision, I must admit, I regret,
But I can't go back.
I came today hoping for open arms 'n' forgiveness as a father;
But I was wrong.
Instead finding a new lesson; with you my teacher.
Son: When I was young I hoped for this day,
Yet, I thought it would go a different way.
There was a time I missed you.
I pictured you in memories as if you were there;
Fishin, ridin a bike, shit that fathers 'n' sons normally share.
I open our box of memories 'n' find just one old photo.
It still lays there, 'n' otherwise empty,
Hoping one day my father will come back to me.

I'm blind 'n' I try to seek out shelter,
Not harbor this anger 'n' pain, but maintain peace at mind.
Yet, my souls heavy out weighin the feather,
'N' even when the clouds scatter my heart still rains.
But don't you turn your back on me yet,
I'll come out stronger;
A new 'n' better man.
I try 'n' keep it together
Whispering, " lord I'm trapped,
'N' even with the sun shining down on me,
I deal wit the weather."
<u>*Child:*</u> *Will our whole life always be a struggle?*
Always strive for something better?
Why must we suffer?
Can't we do something right,
'n' get from under here; a new life?
<u>*Old Man's voice:*</u> *Lord knows I try… Just aint living right.*
Cell door rolls close 'n' I count down years.
Put my past behind me 'n' who I use to be if you'd answer my prayers.
But the crows still stare at me.
Just don't know if they're here to bury me,
Or a reminder of who I use to be.

After marrying, having a son, and creating the life he thought he wanted, Ryan Harnish found himself escaping trouble by turning to drugs and alcohol. His choices led to incarceration in the Illinois Penitentiary System. He now lives near Chicago where he has reunited with his son.